Let's Enjoy Mast

Sense and Sensibility
理性與感性

WORDS 1000

Original Author Jane Austen
Adaptor Michael Robert Bradie
Illustrator An Ji-yeon

MP3

Let's Enjoy Masterpieces!

All the beautiful fairy tales and masterpieces that you have encountered during your childhood remain as warm memories in your adulthood. This time, let's indulge in the world of masterpieces through English. You can enjoy the depth and beauty of original works, which you can't enjoy through Chinese translations.

The stories are easy for you to understand because of your familiarity with them. When you enjoy reading, your ability to understand English will also rapidly improve.

This series of ***Let's Enjoy Masterpieces*** is a special reading comprehension booster program, devised to improve reading comprehension for beginners whose command of English is not satisfactory, or who are elementary, middle, and high school students. With this program, you can enjoy reading masterpieces in English with fun and efficiency.

This carefully planned program is composed of 5 levels, from the beginner level of 350 words to the intermediate and advanced levels of 1,000 words. With this program's level-by-level system, you are able to read famous texts in English and to savor the true pleasure of the world's language.

The program is well conceived, composed of reader-friendly explanations of English expressions and grammar, quizzes to help the student learn vocabulary and understand the meaning of the texts, and fabulous illustrations that adorn every page. In addition, with our "Guide to Listening," not only is reading comprehension enhanced but also listening comprehension skills are highlighted.

In the audio recording of the book, texts are vividly read by professional American actors. The texts are rewritten, according to the levels of the readers by an expert editorial staff of native speakers, on the basis of standard American English with the ministry of education recommended vocabulary. Therefore, it will be of great help even for all the students that want to learn English.

Please indulge yourself in the fun of reading and listening to English through ***Let's Enjoy Masterpieces***.

Introduction

珍・奧斯汀 Jane Austen (1775–1817)

Jane Austen was born on December 16th, 1775, in the village of Steventon, Hampshire, England. She was the seventh child (out of eight) and the second daughter (out of two) of the Reverend George Austen and his wife, Cassandra Leigh. Jane Austen had a happy childhood with her sister, brothers, and the other children who lodged with the family and whom Mr. Austen tutored. Mr. Austen had an extensive library. As a little girl, Jane was often encouraged to read and write.

Ever since her books were first published, (*Sense and Sensibility* in 1811, *Pride and Prejudice* in 1813, *Mansfield Park* in 1814, and *Emma* in 1815), they have been frequently reprinted.

Her novels are admired because they carefully describe the problems of love and marriage between common people in the British middle-class during her lifetime. Unfortunately, she died in 1817 at the age of 42. Her posthumous novels *Northanger Abbey and Persuasion* were published at the end of 1817.

Though not the first novel she wrote, ***Sense and Sensibility*** was the first Jane Austen published under the pseudonym "A Lady." The novel was originally titled *Elinor and Marianne*. Its background is England during the 18th century. It describes the love and conflicts related to the marriages of the Dashwood sisters, Elinor and Marianne. Elinor represents the "sense" of the title, and Marianne represents "sensibility" of the title. The novel shows how the two sisters become mature through some difficult experiences.

The Dashwoods live in Norland Park, England. Mrs. Dashwood is Mr. Dashwood's second wife. She and her three daughters Elinor, Marianne, and Margaret are facing poverty after the death of her husband. Most of the dead Mr. Dashwood's inheritance is given to John Dashwood, his son from his first marriage. John promised his father that he would take good care of his stepmother and sisters, but his selfish wife Fanny does not allow him to give them their fair share of the inheritance. Mrs. Dashwood and her daughters are treated as unwelcome guests in their former home. Luckily, a distant relative offers to rent the Dashwood women a cottage.

Marianne has Colonel Brandon and Willoughby proposing to marry her. Marianne has no interest in Colonel Brandon who is quiet and in his 30s, but she is in love with Willoughby, who is quite a handsome man. Elinor has long been attracted to Fanny's brother Edward, a quiet young man with a gentle nature. Elinor admires Edward's intelligence and good sense. After the two sisters have experienced both romance and heartbreak, they each find love and happiness.

How to Use This Book

本書使用說明

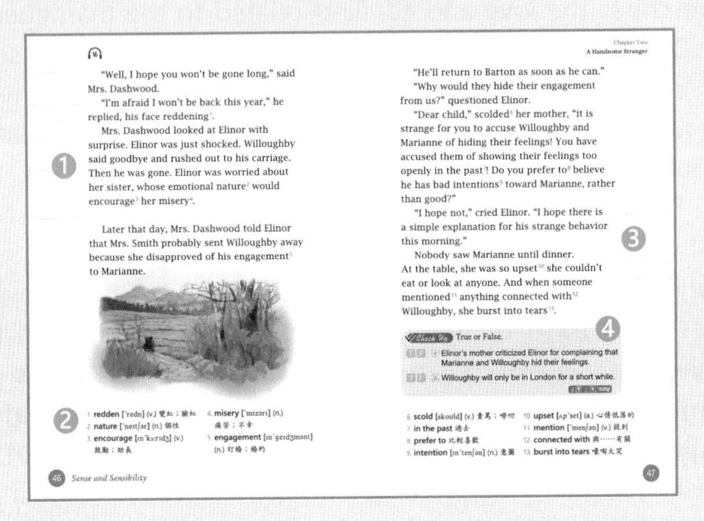

Chapter Two
A Handsome Stranger

"Well, I hope you won't be gone long," said Mrs. Dashwood.

"I'm afraid I won't be back this year," he replied, his face reddening[1].

Mrs. Dashwood looked at Elinor with surprise. Elinor was just shocked. Willoughby said goodbye and rushed out to his carriage. Then he was gone. Elinor was worried about her sister, whose emotional nature[2] would encourage[3] her misery[4].

Later that day, Mrs. Dashwood told Elinor that Mrs. Smith probably sent Willoughby away because she disapproved of his engagement[5] to Marianne.

"He'll return to Barton as soon as he can."

"Why would they hide their engagement from us?" questioned Elinor.

"Dear child," scolded[6] her mother, "it is strange for you to accuse Willoughby and Marianne of hiding their feelings! You have accused them of showing their feelings too openly in the past[7]! Do you prefer to[8] believe he has bad intentions[9] toward Marianne, rather than good?"

"I hope not," cried Elinor. "I hope there is a simple explanation for his strange behavior this morning."

Nobody saw Marianne until dinner. At the table, she was so upset[10] she couldn't eat or look at anyone. And when someone mentioned[11] anything connected with[12] Willoughby, she burst into tears[13].

True or False.

(a) Elinor's mother criticized Elinor for complaining that Marianne and Willoughby hid their feelings.

(b) Willoughby will only be in London for a short while.

1. redden [ˈrɛdn] (v.) 變紅；臉紅
2. nature [ˈneɪtʃər] (n.) 個性
3. encourage [ɪnˈkɜːrɪdʒ] (v.) 鼓勵；助長
4. misery [ˈmɪzəri] (n.) 痛苦；不幸
5. engagement [ɪnˈgeɪdʒmənt] (n.) 訂婚；婚約
6. scold [skould] (v.) 責罵；嘮叨
7. in the past 過去
8. prefer to 比較喜歡
9. intention [ɪnˈtenʃən] (n.) 意圖
10. upset [ʌpˈset] (a.) 心情低落的
11. mention [ˈmenʃən] (v.) 提到
12. connected with 與……有關
13. burst into tears 嚎啕大哭

46 Sense and Sensibility 47

1 Original English texts

It is easy to understand the meaning of the text, because the text is rewritten according to the levels of the readers.

2 Explanation of the vocabulary

The words and expressions that include vocabulary above the elementary level are clearly defined.

3 Response notes

Spaces are included in the book so you can take notes about what you don't understand or what you want to remember.

4 One point lesson

In-depth analyses of major grammar points and expressions help you to understand sentences with difficult grammar.

Audio Recording

In the audio recording, native speakers narrate the texts in standard American English. By combining the written words and the audio recording, you can listen to English with great ease.

Audio books have been popular in Britain and America for many decades. They allow the listener to experience the proper word pronunciation and sentence intonation that add important meaning and drama to spoken English. Students will benefit from listening to the recording twenty or more times.

After you are familiar with the text and recording, listen once more with your eyes closed to check your listening comprehension. Finally, after you can listen with your eyes closed and understand every word and every sentence, you are then ready to mimic the native speaker.

Then you should make a recording by reading the text yourself. Then play both recordings to compare your oral skills with those of a native speaker.

How to Improve Reading Ability

如何增進英文閱讀能力

1 *Catch key words*

Read the key words in the sentences and practice catching the gist of the meaning of the sentence. You might question how working with a few important words could enhance your reading ability. However, it's quite effective. If you continue to use this method, you will find out that the key words and your knowledge of people and situations enables you to understand the sentence.

2 *Divide long sentences*

Read in chunks of meaning, dividing sentences into meaningful chunks of information. In the book, chunks are arranged in sentences according to meaning. If you consider the sentences backwards or grammatically, your reading speed will be slow and you will find it difficult to listen to English.

You are ready to move to a more sophisticated level of comprehension when you find that narrowly focusing on chunks is irritating. Instead of considering the chunks, you will make it a habit to read the sentence from the beginning to the end to figure out the meaning of the whole.

3 Make inferences and assumptions

Making inferences and assumptions is part of your ability. If you don't know, try to guess the meaning of the words. Although you don't know all the words in context, don't go straight to the dictionary. Developing an ability to make inferences in the context is important.

The first way to figure out the meaning of a word is from its context. If you cannot make head or tail out of the meaning of a word, look at what comes before or after it. Ask yourself what can happen in such a situation. Make your best guess as to the word's meaning. Then check the explanations of the word in the book or look up the word in a dictionary.

4 Read a lot and reread the same book many times

There is no shortcut to mastering English. Only if you do a lot of reading will you make your way to the summit. Read fun and easy books with an average of less than one new word per page. Try to immerse yourself in English as often as you can.

Spend time "swimming" in English. Language learning research has shown that immersing yourself in English will help you improve your English, even though you may not be aware of what you're learning.

Before You Read

Elinor

I am Elinor, the oldest of three sisters. Our mother is Mrs. Dashwood, and our father, Henry Dashwood, died suddenly in middle age[1]. I must be strong and take good care of my mother and sisters. I cannot let[2] my own emotions control[3] me, for if I do, I will just be adding to[4] my family's difficulties[5].

Marianne

Oh, when will I meet my true love? I am looking for a handsome, young, gentleman who will sweep me off my feet[6]. It doesn't matter if he is fabulously[7] rich or not. I don't understand my older sister Elinor. It's obvious[8] that she is in love with Edward Ferrars, but she does not show it. Oh, if I were in love, I would show him how much I loved him!

1. **middle age** 中年
2. **let + *A* + 原型動詞**：讓 A……
3. **control** [kən`troʊl] (v.) 控制
4. **add to** 增加
5. **difficulty** [`dɪfɪkəlti] (n.) 困境
6. **sweep sb off sb's feet** 使某人傾心
7. **fabulously** [`fæbjʊləsli] (adv.) 驚人地
8. **obvious** [`ɑːbvɪəs] (a.) 明顯的

Edward Ferrars

I am not a very ambitious[9] man. My family wants me to be a successful man in society, but I just want a simple, private[10] life. Even if I have to give it up[11] to marry the woman I love, I would pursue[12] a quiet life.

Willoughby

I am a charming[13], young, and handsome gentleman. Maybe I am a bit of[14] a playboy. But I don't have a lot of money. So when I marry, it must be to a woman who is rich and who can support[15] me.

Colonel Brandon

I am a quiet man, but I am not timid or shy. I think I have fallen in love with Marianne. However, she recently[16] is in love with Willoughby. I know he is such a scoundrel[17] but I won't say anything about him for the time being[18] because I do not want her to be hurt by anyone.

9. **ambitious** [æm`bɪʃəs] (a.) 有野心的
10. **private** [`praɪvɪt] (a.) 隱私的
11. **give up** 放棄
12. **pursue** [pər`suː] (v.) 追求
13. **charming** [`tʃɑːrmɪŋ] (a.) 迷人的
14. **a bit of** 有點兒
15. **support** [sə`pɔːrt] (v.) 供養；支持
16. **recently** [`riːsəntli] (adv.) 最近
17. **scoundrel** [`skaundrəl] (n.) 渾蛋
18. **for the time being** 目前

The Dashwoods

The Dashwoods[1] lived in the Southern English town of Sussex for many generations[2]. They owned a large country house[3] named[4] Norland Park. The head of the family was old Mr. Dashwood, an elderly[5] unmarried[6] gentleman. During the last years of Mr. Dashwood's life, he invited his nephew[7], Henry Dashwood, and his family to move into Norland Park.

Henry Dashwood had one son, John, by his first wife and three daughters by his present[8] wife. John was a young man who had received a large inheritance[9] from his mother. The Norland fortune[10] was not as important to John as it was to his sisters who had little money of their own.

---

1. **the+family name+s** 集合名詞，同姓氏的一家人
2. **generation** [ˌdʒenəˋreɪʃən] (n.) 世代
3. **country house** 鄉間小屋
4. **named** [neɪmd] (a.) 被命名為……
5. **elderly** [ˋeldərli] (a.) 年長的
6. **unmarried** [ˌʌnˋmærid] (a.) 未婚的
7. **nephew** [ˋnefjuː] (n.) 姪子

When old Mr. Dashwood died, Henry learned that his uncle had not left the fortune to him, but rather for him to use during his lifetime[11]. When Henry died, the inheritance would pass to his son John and then to John's son. This was because old Mr. Dashwood had been especially fond of[12] John's son. But out of kindness, the old man left Henry's daughters 1,000 pounds each.

Check Up

Why did old Mr. Dashwood not leave all his money to Henry?

a He was very impressed with his nephew's grandson.

b He did not like Henry's daughters.

c He wanted to give all the money to John instead.

Ans: a

8. **present** [`prezənt] (a.) 現任的
9. **inheritance** [ɪn`herɪtəns] (n.) 遺產；資產
10. **fortune** [`fɔːrtʃən] (n.) 財富
11. **lifetime** [`laɪftaɪm] (n.) 一生
12. **be fond of** 喜愛……

2

Henry wanted the fortune for his wife and daughters. But if he invested[1] his money carefully, he would have enough to provide for[2] them. Unfortunately[3], Henry suddenly died, unable to complete his plan. At this time[4], all that was left for his wife and daughters was 10,000 pounds.

Shortly before his death, Henry begged his son John to take care of his stepmother[5] and sisters. John did not have strong feelings for them, but he promised he would make them comfortable[6]. He was not a bad man, but he was selfish[7] and cold-hearted[8]. His wife Fanny was even more selfish and cold-hearted than him.

As soon as Henry was buried[9], Fanny came to Norland Park uninvited[10]. She rudely[11] informed[12] Mrs. Dashwood and her daughters that Norland Park was now hers and that they were her guests.

---

1. **invest** [ɪn`vest] (v.) 投資
2. **provide for** 撫養；供給
3. **unfortunately** [ʌn`fɔːrtʃənətli] (adv.) 不幸地
4. **at this time** 這次；此時
5. **stepmother** [`stepmʌðər] (n.) 繼母
6. **comfortable** [`kʌmfərtəbəl] (a.) 舒適的
7. **selfish** [`selfɪʃ] (a.) 自私的
8. **cold-hearted** [`kould`hɑːrtɪd] (a.) 心腸冷酷的

The recently widowed[13] Mrs. Dashwood was terribly offended[14]. She would have left the estate[15] immediately[16] if her eldest daughter had not begged her to reconsider[17].

Elinor was the eldest daughter. She possessed[18] great intelligence and common sense[19]. She was only nineteen, but she frequently advised her mother on important matters.

9. **bury** [\`beri] (v.) 埋葬
10. **uninvited** [ˏʌnɪn\`vaɪtɪd] (a.) 沒被邀請的
11. **rudely** [\`ruːdli] (adv.) 無禮地
12. **inform** [ɪn\`fɔːrm] (v.) 通知
13. **widowed** [\`wɪdoud] (a.) 寡婦的
14. **offend** [ə\`fend] (v.) 冒犯
15. **estate** [ɪ\`steɪt] (n.) 莊園；地產
16. **immediately** [ɪ\`miːdiətli] (adv.) 立刻
17. **reconsider** [ˏriːkən\`sɪdər] (v.) 再考慮
18. **possess** [pə\`zes] (v.) 擁有
19. **common sense** 常識

Elinor had an excellent sense of self-control[1], which her mother and her younger sister Marianne lacked[2].

Like Elinor, Marianne was generous[3], clever, and sensitive[4]. But she had very strong emotions[5], which she was unable to hide. She was much like her mother.

The youngest sister Margaret was a sweet thirteen-year old who shared Marianne's emotional[6] sensibility[7] but none of her intelligence.

One day, John Dashwood reminded his wife of[8] the promise[9] he had made to his dying father and said he wanted to give each of his sisters 1,000 pounds. However, Fanny disapproved of[10] this gift[11].

1. **self-control** [self kən`trəul] (n.) 自制
2. **lack** [læk] (v.) 欠缺
3. **generous** [`dʒenərəs] (a.) 大方的；慷慨的
4. **sensitive** [`sensətɪv] (a.) 敏感的
5. **emotion** [ɪ`mouʃən] (n.) 情緒
6. **emotional** [ɪ`mouʃənəl] (a.) 情緒化的
7. **sensibility** [sensɪ`bɪlɪti] (n.) 感受力

"You'll be taking 3,000 pounds out of our son's future inheritance," she said. "And you're only related to[12] them by half blood. They are hardly even your sisters."

"I must do something for them when they leave Norland for a new home. Perhaps I should give them 500 pounds each," replied John.

"That's too much," argued[13] Fanny. "You're very generous, but I think they'll be able to live very comfortably on the 10,000 pounds your father left them."

"That's true," replied John. "Why don't I just give my stepmother 100 pounds every year?"

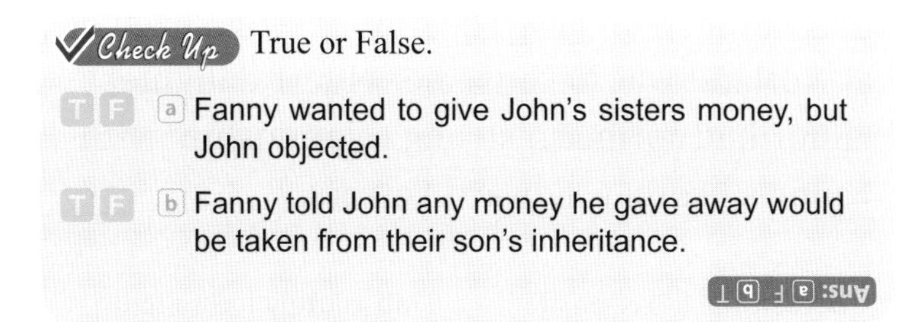

8. **remind *A* of** 提醒 A
9. **promise** [ˋprɑmɪs] (n.) 承諾
10. **disapprove of** 不贊成
11. **gift** [gɪft] (n.) 禮物；贈予
12. **related to** 有關係的；與……是親戚
13. **argue** [ˋɑːrgjuː] (v.) 爭論

4

"Yes, but I don't think your father meant for you to give them any money at all," replied Fanny. "I think he wanted you to find them a small, comfortable house to live in, to help them move, and perhaps to send them an occasional[1] basket of fish or meat. They don't need a carriage[2] or horses, and only one or two servants[3]. It would be foolish to give them any more."

"I think you're absolutely[4] right," said John. "Now I understand what my father meant."

He decided to offer the assistance[5] his wife suggested.

Meanwhile[6] Henry's widow[7], Mrs. Dashwood, wanted to leave Norland as soon as possible. Mrs. Dashwood had come to[8] strongly dislike her daughter-in-law. The only reason she stayed at Norland was because her eldest daughter Elinor had formed a strong relationship[9] with Fanny's brother, Edward Ferrars.

---

1. **occasional** [ə`keɪʒənəl] (a.) 偶爾的
2. **carriage** [`kærɪdʒ] (n.) 四輪馬車
3. **servant** [`sɜːrvənt] (n.) 僕人
4. **absolutely** [ˌæbsə`luːtli] (adv.) 絕對地
5. **assistance** [ə`sɪstəns] (n.) 幫助
6. **meanwhile** [`miːnwaɪl] (adv.) 同一時刻

Edward's father had died and left behind[10] a lot of money. But Edward was not sure if he would receive the large inheritance. It depended on[11] his mother's wishes[12]. But Mrs. Dashwood didn't care about his money. He and her daughter seemed to love each other.

7. **widow** [ˋwɪdoʊ] (n.) 寡婦
8. **come to** 達到
9. **relationship** [rɪˋleɪʃənʃɪp] (n.) 關聯；戀愛關係
10. **leave behind** 遺留下
11. **depend on** 仰賴；取決於
12. **wish** [wɪʃ] (n.) 想法

One Point Lesson

- Mrs. Dashwood had come to strongly dislike her **daughter-in-law.** 戴西伍夫人對媳婦非常反感。

---

in-law：法律上的

e.g. father-in-law 公公、岳父　mother-in-law 婆婆、岳母
sister-in-law 大姑、小姑、大姨子、小姨、嫂嫂、弟媳
brother-in-law 大伯、小叔、姊夫、妹夫、連襟

5

Edward Ferrars was not handsome or especially gentlemanly[1]. He was shy with a kind heart. His mother and sister wanted him to be a great man in society, but he was not ambitious. All he wanted were the comforts[2] and quietness[3] of private life. His younger brother Robert had greater potential[4].

"Edward and Elinor will most likely[5] be married in a few months," Mrs. Dashwood told Marianne. "Don't you approve of[6] Edward?"

1. **gentlemanly** [`dʒentlmənli] (a.) 紳士的
2. **comfort** [`kʌmfərt] (n.) 舒適
3. **quietness** [`kwaɪətnɪs] (n.) 平靜
4. **potential** [pə`tenʃəl] (n.) 潛力
5. **likely** [`laɪkli] (adv.) 可能地
6. **approve of** 贊同
7. **taste** [teɪst] (n.) 品味

"He has no fire in his eyes. He doesn't seem to have any taste[7] in books or music. Oh, how will I ever find a man I can truly love?" worried Marianne.

"You're only seventeen," laughed Mrs. Dashwood. "It's too early for you to lose hope."

Elinor had a very high opinion of Edward, but she was not sure she wanted to marry him. He often seemed strangely depressed[8]. And she feared he thought of her only as a friend.

But Marianne and her mother had no such doubts. They believed love could solve all problems. Marianne thought it was terrible when her sister described[9] her feelings for Edward as respect rather than[10] love.

"Like him? Respect him? Oh, cold-hearted Elinor! Why are you ashamed to[11] express your love?"

Check Up

What is the best way to describe Marianne's opinion of Edward?

a. He is a bold, courageous man.

b. He is full of life.

c. He is a lifeless bore.

Ans: c

8. **depressed** [dɪ`prest] (a.) 沮喪的

9. **describe** [dɪ`skraɪb] (v.) 形容

10. **rather than** 而不是……

11. **be ashamed to** 對……感到羞愧

6

Fanny also noticed the attachment[1] between her brother and Elinor. It made her uneasy[2]. She told her mother-in-law, Mrs. Dashwood, "My mother and I expect Edward to marry well. It would be dangerous for Elinor to try and trap[3] Edward into marrying her."

This made Mrs. Dashwood furious[4]. She decided that she and her daughters must leave Norland immediately.

On that same day, she received a letter from a distant[5] relative[6] of hers named Sir John Middleton. He wrote to offer her a small house near his estate in Devonshire. His letter was so welcoming[7] that Mrs. Dashwood wrote a letter to accept his offer[8] right away.

Mrs. Dashwood was happy to inform John and Fanny that she and her daughters would be leaving Norland to live in Devonshire.

1. **attachment** [ə`tætʃmənt] (n.) 情感
2. **uneasy** [ʌn`i:zi] (a.) 不安的
3. **trap** [træp] (v.) 設下陷阱引誘
4. **furious** [`fjʊriəs] (a.) 憤怒的
5. **distant** [`dɪstənt] (a.) 遙遠的
6. **relative** [`relətɪv] (n.) 親戚
7. **welcoming** [`welkəmɪŋ] (a.) 歡迎的
8. **offer** [`ɑ:fər] (n.) 提供

Edward Ferrars, who was in the room at that time, turned quickly toward her and said, "Devonshire! That's so far from here."

"Yes," she replied. "We'll be in Barton, four miles from the city of Exeter. It's only a cottage[9], but I hope you'll all visit us there."

Mrs. Dashwood's invitation[10] to Edward was very affectionate[11], as she did not want to discourage[12] his relationship with her Elinor.

9. **cottage** [ˋkɑːtɪdʒ] (n.) 農舍；小屋
10. **invitation** [ˌɪnvɪˋteɪʃən] (n.) 邀請
11. **affectionate** [əˋfekʃənət] (a.) 溫柔親切的
12. **discourage** [dɪsˋkɜːrɪdʒ] (v.) 使……洩氣；阻擋

7

Barton Cottage was furnished[1] and ready for them to move in at once[2]. Elinor recommended her mother to sell their carriage and horses and to have only three servants.

On his deathbed[3], Henry had told his wife of John's promise to care for[4] her and her daughters. But as they left, it looked as if John would not offer any assistance. In fact, John was heard to complain about money and how he was in need of[5] more himself.

The sisters cried when they said goodbye to their beloved[6] home Norland. "Dear, dear Norland," cried Marianne while walking alone in the park on their last evening, "I will miss you for the rest of my life!"

During their journey[7] to Devonshire, the sisters were too miserable[8] to enjoy the trip. But as they entered Barton Valley, they became more cheerful[9]. They took notice of[10] the countryside where they would live. Barton Valley consisted of[11] thick woods, clear streams, and expansive[12] open fields.

---

1. **furnished** [ˋfɜːrnɪʃt] (a.) 有傢俱的
2. **at once** 立刻
3. **on one's deathbed** 某人臨終的一段時間
4. **care for** 照料

Barton Cottage was in excellent condition[13]. There were two sitting rooms[14], four bedrooms, and two servant's quarters[15]. It was much smaller and poorer than Norland, but the girls made their best efforts[16] to be happy.

5. **in need of** 需要……
6. **beloved** [bɪ`lʌvɪd] (a.) 摯愛的
7. **journey** [`dʒɜːrni] (n.) 旅程
8. **miserable** [`mɪzərəbəl] (a.) 悲哀的
9. **cheerful** [`tʃɪrfəl] (a.) 情緒好的；愉快的
10. **take notice of** 注意
11. **consist of** 由……組成
12. **expansive** [ɪk`spænsɪv] (a.) 廣闊的
13. **condition** [kən`dɪʃən] (n.) 情況
14. **sitting room** 起居室；客廳
15. **servants' quarter** 傭人住處
16. **make one's effort** 努力

8

The next day, the Dashwoods received a visit from their landlord[1], Sir John Middleton. He was a good-looking[2], cheerful man. He welcomed them and offered them anything from his house and garden. His house was called Barton Park. He tried to make them as comfortable as possible and said he hoped they would come and visit his family soon.

---

1. **landlord** [`lændlɔrd] (n.) 房東；地主
2. **good-looking** 好看的
3. **stately** [`steɪtli] (a.) 高貴的；堂皇的
4. **in comfort** 舒服地
5. **spoil** [spɔɪl] (v.) 溺愛
6. **hospitable** [`hɑːspɪtəbəl] (a.) 好客的；周到的
7. **be famous for** 以……著名
8. **apologize** [ə`pɑːlədʒaɪz] (v.) 道歉
9. **colonel** [`kɜːrnəl] (n.) 上校

They went to Barton Park for dinner the next day. The estate was half a mile from their cottage. It was a large, stately[3] house, where the Middletons lived in great comfort[4]. Sir John was a sportsman who enjoyed shooting, while Lady Middleton was a mother who spoiled[5] her children.

Sir John was a hospitable[6] man and always had relatives or friends staying at their house. The noisier and more full of young people, the better. Barton Park was famous for[7] its summer parties and winter dances.

On the night the Dashwoods arrived for dinner, Sir John apologized[8] that there were no handsome young male guests to meet them. The only guests were Colonel[9] Brandon, a friend staying at the house, and Sir John's mother-in-law, Mrs. Jennings.

One Point Lesson

The noisier and more full of young people, **the better.**
越多人越吵就越好。

the + 比較級，the 比較級：越……就越……

e.g. **The more** you get, **the more** you want.
得到的越多，想要的也越多。

9

Mrs. Jennings was a fat, cheerful old lady who talked and laughed a great deal[1]. Colonel Brandon was silent, serious, and handsome. Elinor and Marianne noticed he was an old bachelor[2], on the wrong side of[3] thirty-five.

After dinner, Marianne sang and played the piano. While Sir John was loud in showing his delight[4] for the music, Colonel Brandon was quiet and listened attentively[5].

1. **a great deal** 很多地
2. **bachelor** [ˋbætʃələr] (n.) 單身男子
3. **on the wrong side of** 已過……歲
4. **delight** [dɪˋlaɪt] (n.) 樂趣
5. **attentively** [əˋtentɪvli] (adv.) 專心地
6. **comfortable** [ˋkʌmftərbəl] (a.) 寬裕的；豐富的

Mrs. Jennings was a widow with a comfortable[6] fortune. She had seen both of her daughters marry respectably[7] and now had nothing better to do than to try and marry off[8] the rest of the world. She spent a lot of time matching young people with one another[9] and planning their weddings.

Mrs. Jennings informed the Middletons and the Dashwoods that Colonel Brandon was very much in love with[10] Marianne. She felt it would be an excellent marriage because he was rich and she was beautiful.

"How cruel[11] for Mrs. Jennings to say that," remarked[12] Marianne. "Colonel Brandon is old enough to be my father!"

"But I cannot think of a man five years younger than me being as ancient as you say," replied Mrs. Dashwood.

"But didn't you hear him complaining of his bad back?" said Marianne.

7. **respectably** [rɪ`spektəbli] (adv.) 體面地
8. **marry off** 把……嫁出去
9. **one another** 彼此
10. **be in love with** 愛上……
11. **cruel** [`kru:əl] (a.) 殘忍的；傷人的
12. **remark** [rɪ`mɑ:rk] (v.) 說；評論

10

"My child," laughed Mrs. Dashwood. "It must seem amazing to you that I've lived to the great age of forty. Thirty-five has nothing to do with[1] marriage. For example, a woman of twenty-seven could easily consider marrying a man of Colonel Brandon's age."

"But a woman of twenty-seven could consider becoming his nurse if her house is uncomfortable[2] and her fortune is small. It would be a marriage of convenience[3]."

"It seems a little hard," remarked Elinor, "to accuse Colonel Brandon of needing nursing[4] just because he complained of a pain in his shoulder on a cold, wet day."

But Marianne's view[5] about the colonel did not change. After Elinor left the room, Marianne said, "Mother, I'm concerned about[6] Edward Ferrars. I'm worried he is sick. We've been here two weeks, and he hasn't come to see Elinor."

1. **have nothing to do with** 與……無關
2. **uncomfortable** [ʌn`kʌmfərtəbəl] (a.) 不舒服的
3. **convenience** [kən`vi:niəns] (n.) 方便
4. **nursing** [`nɜ:rsɪŋ] (n.) 照顧
5. **view** [vju:] (n.) 觀點
6. **be concerned about** 在意；掛慮

"Be patient[7], my daughter," Mrs. Dashwood answered. "I don't expect him so soon. And Elinor doesn't, either."

"It is so strange," exclaimed[8] Marianne, "How cold and calm their last goodbyes were! Elinor is so self-controlled, never sad or restless[9] or miserable. I don't understand her."

Check Up

Why doesn't Marianne want to marry Colonel Brandon?

a She doesn't think he is handsome.

b She is afraid of becoming his nurse.

c She loves someone else.

Ans: b

7. **patient** [ˋpeɪʃənt] (a.) 有耐心的

8. **exclaim** [ɪkˋskleɪm] (v.) 呼喊；驚叫

9. **restless** [ˋrestləs] (a.) 焦躁不安的；靜不下來的

A Match.

1. Marianne Dashwood •
2. Elinor Dashwood •
3. John Dashwood •
4. Edward Ferrars •
5. Colonel Brandon •

- • a was selfish and cold-hearted.
- • b had no fire in his eyes.
- • c possessed great intelligence and common sense.
- • d was an old bachelor on the wrong side of 35.
- • e had strong emotions and was unable to hide them.

B Fill in the blanks with proper words.

inheritance widowed generations fond ambitious

1. The Dashwoods lived in Sussex for many ___________.
2. John received a large ___________ from his mother.
3. Old Mr. Dashwood had been especially ___________ of John's son.
4. The recently ___________ Mrs. Dashwood was terribly offended by her daughter-in-law.
5. Edward's mother wanted him to be a great man, but he was not ___________.

C Choose the correct answer.

1. What did Fanny warn that Mrs. Dashwood would be dangerous?
   (a) That Mrs. Dashwood and her daughters continued to live in Norland.
   (b) That John Dashwood gave his stepmother and sisters 1,000 pounds each.
   (c) That Mrs. Dashwood's eldest daughter tried to "catch" her brother, Edward.

2. How did Colonel Brandon feel about Marianne?
   (a) He fell in love with her.
   (b) He wanted to marry her because she was rich.
   (c) He strongly disliked her because she didn't like him.

D True or False.

T F 1. Henry Dashwood made his son promise to find husbands for Marianne and Elinor.

T F 2. Mrs. Dashwood had a lot of money from a business she owned.

T F 3. Marianne thought Colonel Brandon was old enough to be her father.

T F 4. Mrs. Jennings was a fat, cheerful old lady who talked a lot.

Chapter Two

11 A Handsome Stranger

The Dashwood sisters were finally beginning to feel comfortable at Barton Cottage. They enjoyed taking walks[1] and practicing music for the first time since their father died. They didn't have many visitors, and there were few other houses within walking distance[2]. The only nearby place was a large mansion[3], Allenham, a mile away. They heard the owner was an old lady named Mrs. Smith, who wasn't well enough to have visitors.

One day, despite[4] Elinor's warning[5] of rain, Marianne and Margaret walked up a hill behind the cottage. At the top, they were delighted at[6] the blue sky and white clouds. They laughed as the wind blew their hair, and Marianne cried, "This is the greatest place in the world!"

---

1. **take a walk** 散步
2. **within walking distance** 在走路可到的距離內
3. **mansion** [`mænʃən] (n.) 宅第；大廈
4. **despite** [dɪ`spaɪt] (prep.) 儘管

But within minutes, dark clouds rolled in[7] and rain poured down[8]. The girls ran down the hill as fast as they could. Margaret was ahead and didn't see Marianne slip[9] and fall.

At this time, a gentleman out hunting saw her accident[10] and ran to help her. Her ankle was twisted[11], so she couldn't stand. The gentleman carried her to Barton Cottage. There he placed her on the sofa.

5. **warning** [ˋwɔːrnɪŋ] (n.) 警告
6. **be delighted at** 開心於……
7. **roll in** 大量湧進
8. **pour down** 傾瀉而下
9. **slip** [slɪp] (v.) 滑跤；失足
10. **accident** [ˋæksɪdənt] (n.) 意外
11. **twist** [twɪst] (v.) 扭

12

Elinor and her mother were shocked when the stranger entered the house carrying Marianne. They both noticed his handsome appearance[1]. He apologized for a rude entrance[2], and Mrs. Dashwood expressed her gratitude[3] for his helping Marianne.

She asked his name. It was Willoughby. He presently lived at Allenham. He said he would visit them tomorrow to check on[4] Marianne. Mrs. Dashwood said he would always be welcome at the cottage. Then he left into the pouring rain.

---

1. **appearance** [ə`pɪrəns] (n.) 外表
2. **entrance** [`entrəns] (n.) 進入
3. **gratitude** [`grætɪtu:d] (n.) 感激
4. **check on** 檢查
5. **admire** [əd`maɪr] (v.) 欣賞
6. **barely** [`berli] (adv.) 幾乎不
7. **due to** 由於

Elinor and her mother admired[5] the man, but Marianne had barely[6] seen him due to[7] her condition. She imagined her hero so intensely[8] that she didn't feel the pain of her injured[9] ankle.

When Sir John visited them, he was asked if he knew Willoughby of Allenham.

"Willoughby! Of course!" he exclaimed. "He visits us every year. I shall invite him to dinner on Thursday."

"What sort of man is he?" asked Mrs. Dashwood.

"He's a good man. He shoots well, and he's the best horseman[10] in England."

They demanded[11] more personal details. Sir John told them Willoughby had no house in Devonshire. He stayed with his relative, Mrs. Smith, at Allenham when he visited. He also said Willoughby would probably inherit[12] the old lady's fortune.

---

8. **intensely** [ɪn`tensli] (adv.) 熱切地；緊張地
9. **injured** [`ɪndʒərd] (a.) 受傷的
10. **horseman** [`hɔːrsmæn] (n.) 騎士
11. **demand** [dɪ`mænd] (v.) 要求；請求
12. **inherit** [ɪn`herɪt] (v.) 繼承

13

Marianne's rescuer[1] visited the next morning. Willoughby became very comfortable with the Dashwoods. The fire in Marianne's eyes seemed to draw him in[2]. They shared many interests[3] and spoke without shyness[4]. By the end of his visit, they talked like old friends.

Willoughby visited Barton Cottage every day afterward. At first, he pretended to worry about Marianne's health. But he soon stopped pretending and openly enjoyed Marianne's company[5]. They read and sang and talked together.

1. **rescuer** [ˋreskjuːr] (n.) 救援者
2. **draw in** 吸引
3. **interest** [ˋɪntrest] (n.) 興趣
4. **shyness** [ʃaɪnɪs] (n.) 害羞；膽怯
5. **company** [ˋkʌmpəni] (n.) 陪伴
6. **congratulate** [kənˋgrætʃəleɪt] (v.) 恭喜
7. **pity** [ˋpɪti] (v.) 同情
8. **compete for** 爭取
9. **affection** [əˋfekʃən] (n.) 感情
10. **take pleasure in** 享受於……
11. **laugh at** 嘲笑
12. **companion** [kəmˋpænjən] (n.) 同伴；朋友

Marianne thought Willoughby possessed all of the sensibility and taste Edward Ferrars lacked. Soon after, she came to believe that he was perfect for her. Willoughby seemed to feel the same way. Mrs. Dashwood secretly congratulated[6] herself on a great future son-in-law.

Meanwhile, Elinor began to pity[7] Colonel Brandon, who couldn't compete for[8] Marianne's affection[9] with a young man of twenty-five. It bothered Elinor that Marianne and Willoughby took pleasure in[10] laughing at[11] Brandon.

Elinor was not as happy. She found no companion[12] to take her mind away from missing her friends in Sussex. The only person she could talk to was Colonel Brandon, who liked talking about Marianne.

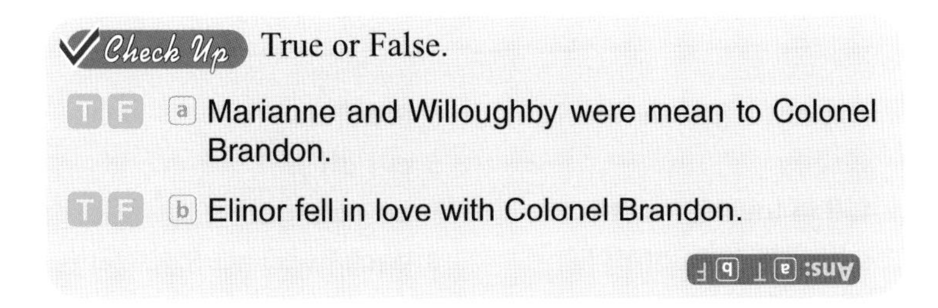
Check Up True or False.

T F a Marianne and Willoughby were mean to Colonel Brandon.

T F b Elinor fell in love with Colonel Brandon.

Ans: a T b F

"I see your sister is not fond of second attachments," said Brandon.

"All of her opinions are romantic[1]. She believes we only fall in love[2] once in our lives. I hope she'll become more sensible[3]."

"That may happen," continued[4] Brandon. "I knew a young lady once who . . ."

He suddenly stopped, thinking he had said too much. Elinor felt sure that his story was of disappointed love. Her pity for him grew.

1. **romantic** [rou`mæntɪk] (a.) 浪漫的
2. **fall in love** 墜入情網
3. **sensible** [`sensəbəl] (a.) 理智的
4. **continue** [kən`tɪnjuː] (v.) 繼續說
5. **lock** [lɑːk] (n.) 一綹
6. **cut off** 剪下
7. **be engaged** 訂婚
8. **pack** [pæk] (v.) 包裝；打包

The next day, Margaret said to Elinor, "I have a secret! Last night I saw Willoughby begging Marianne for a lock[5] of hair. She cut it off[6] and gave it to him. He kissed it and put it in his pocket."

Elinor guessed they were now secretly engaged[7]. She was surprised they had not told anybody.

The following day, Sir John planned a trip for everyone to a house called Whitwell, owned by Colonel Brandon's brother-in-law. A large group of them packed[8] picnic lunches and prepared to leave.

Check Up

At the time when the story takes place, what does it mean when a young lady gives a man a lock of her hair?

ⓐ It's a parting gift meaning "farewell."
ⓑ It usually means that the woman agrees to marry the man.
ⓒ It means that the woman is wishing the man good luck on his journey.

Ans: b

15

But as the people ate breakfast, a letter came for the colonel. He looked at it and explained to the group that he had urgent[1] business.

Their excursion[2] was canceled. They tried to convince him to[3] put off[4] his business, but he wouldn't.

After Brandon left, they decided to ride around the countryside. Marianne got into Willoughby's carriage, and the two were not seen for the rest of the day.

The next morning, Mrs. Dashwood went to visit Lady Middleton with two of her daughters. Marianne stayed home since Willoughby would be coming for a visit.

When Mrs. Dashwood and her daughters returned home, they were not surprised to find Willoughby's carriage in front of the cottage.

1. **urgent** [`ɜ:rdʒənt] (a.) 緊急的
2. **excursion** [ɪk`skɜ:rʒən] (n.) 短程旅行
3. **convince *A* to** 說服 A 去……
4. **put off** 延後；拖延
5. **rush out of** 衝出
6. **sob** [sɑ:b] (v.) 啜泣
7. **uncontrollably** [͵ʌnkən`troʊləbəli] (adv.) 控制不住地
8. **upstairs** [͵ʌp`sterz] (adv.) 往樓上地
9. **on business** 為公事

They went inside, and Marianne came rushing out of[5] the sitting room, sobbing[6] uncontrollably[7]. Then she ran upstairs[8].

Mrs. Dashwood asked Willoughby, "Is she ill?"

"No," he answered, trying to look cheerful, "but I have bad news. My cousin, Mrs. Smith, has sent me to London on business[9]. I won't be able to visit any more. I'm poor and depend on Mrs. Smith. I must do as she asks. I've come to say goodbye."

16

"Well, I hope you won't be gone long," said Mrs. Dashwood.

"I'm afraid I won't be back this year," he replied, his face reddening[1].

Mrs. Dashwood looked at Elinor with surprise. Elinor was just shocked. Willoughby said goodbye and rushed out to his carriage. Then he was gone. Elinor was worried about her sister, whose emotional nature[2] would encourage[3] her misery[4].

Later that day, Mrs. Dashwood told Elinor that Mrs. Smith probably sent Willoughby away because she disapproved of his engagement[5] to Marianne.

1. **redden** [`redn] (v.) 變紅；臉紅
2. **nature** [`neɪtʃər] (n.) 個性
3. **encourage** [ɪn`kɜːrɪdʒ] (v.) 鼓勵；助長
4. **misery** [`mɪzəri] (n.) 痛苦；不幸
5. **engagement** [ɪn`geɪdʒmənt] (n.) 訂婚；婚約

"He'll return to Barton as soon as he can."

"Why would they hide their engagement from us?" questioned Elinor.

"Dear child," scolded[6] her mother, "it is strange for you to accuse Willoughby and Marianne of hiding their feelings! You have accused them of showing their feelings too openly in the past[7]! Do you prefer to[8] believe he has bad intentions[9] toward Marianne, rather than good?"

"I hope not," cried Elinor. "I hope there is a simple explanation for his strange behavior this morning."

Nobody saw Marianne until dinner. At the table, she was so upset[10] she couldn't eat or look at anyone. And when someone mentioned[11] anything connected with[12] Willoughby, she burst into tears[13].

Check Up True or False.

T F (a) Elinor's mother criticized Elinor for complaining that Marianne and Willoughby hid their feelings.

T F (b) Willoughby will only be in London for a short while.

Ans: (a) T (b) F

6. **scold** [skould] (v.) 責罵；嘮叨
7. **in the past** 過去
8. **prefer to** 比較喜歡
9. **intention** [ɪn`tenʃən] (n.) 意圖
10. **upset** [ʌp`set] (a.) 心情低落的
11. **mention** [`menʃən] (v.) 提到
12. **connected with** 與……有關
13. **burst into tears** 嚎啕大哭

17

As the days passed, Marianne got worse and worse. A week later, her sisters persuaded her to[1] go for a walk[2]. While walking, they saw a gentleman riding toward them.

"It's Willoughby! I know it is!" cried Marianne. She ran toward the carriage.

It was not Willoughby but Edward Ferrars, the only person in the world she could forgive[3] for not being Willoughby. She stopped and smiled, holding back[4] her tears. As Edward and Elinor exchanged[5] greetings[6], Marianne saw their polite yet distant[7] behavior.

When they returned to the cottage, Mrs. Dashwood greeted Edward warmly.

"So, Edward, what are your mother's plans for you these days[8]? Does she still want you to be a politician[9]?"

"No," replied Edward, "She knows I could never do that. We'll never agree on[10] a profession[11] for me. I've always wanted to work for the Church. But that's too ordinary[12] for my family."

---

1. **persuade *A* to** 說服 A 做……
2. **go for a walk** 散心
3. **forgive** [fər`giv] (v.) 原諒；寬恕
4. **hold back** 抑制
5. **exchange** [ɪks`tʃeɪndʒ] (v.) 交換
6. **greeting** [`gri:tɪŋ] (n.) 打招呼；問候
7. **distant** [`dɪstənt] (a.) 疏遠的；遙遠的

"I know you're not ambitious, Edward," said Mrs. Dashwood.

"No. I wish to be like everybody else, to be perfectly happy in my own way. Greatness[13] won't make me happy."

"You're right!" cried Marianne. "What does wealth[14] or greatness have to do with[15] happiness?"

"Greatness has very little to do with it," said Elinor, "but wealth has much to do with it."

---

8. **these days** 這些日子
9. **politician** [ˌpɑːlə`tɪʃən] (n.) 政治家
10. **agree on** 同意
11. **profession** [prə`feʃən] (n.) 職業
12. **ordinary** [`ɔːrdəneri] (a.) 普通的；平凡的
13. **greatness** [`greɪtnɪs] (n.) 著名；偉大
14. **wealth** [welθ] (n.) 財富
15. **have to do with** 和……有關

"Elinor!" cried Marianne, "Money only gives happiness where there is nothing else to give it. Beyond[1] answering our basic needs[2], it's of no use[3] at all."

"How much do you need for your basic needs?" asked Elinor.

"Two thousand per year," said Marianne. "No more than that."

Elinor laughed, "Two thousand! One thousand a year would be wealthy[4] to me."

"A family cannot live on[5] less than[6] two thousand per year," said Marianne. "It takes that much to have enough servants, plus[7] a carriage and horses for riding."

Elinor smiled at her sister's description[8] of her future life with Willoughby.

1. **beyond** [bɪˋjɑːnd] (prep.) 此外
2. **needs** [niːdz] (n.) 需求
3. **of no use** 無用處的
4. **wealthy** [ˋwelθi] (a.) 富有的
5. **live on** 靠……生活
6. **less than** 少於
7. **plus** [plʌs] (prep.) 加上
8. **description** [dɪˋskrɪpʃən] (n.) 描述
9. **politeness** [pəˋlaɪtnəs] (n.) 禮儀
10. **alarmed** [əˋlɑːrmd] (a.) 警覺的
11. **coldness** [ˋkouldnəs] (n.) 冷漠
12. **doubt** [daʊt] (v.) 懷疑
13. **blush** [blʌʃ] (v.) 臉紅

During Edward's visit, Elinor showed her usual politeness[9] and interest. But she was alarmed[10] by his coldness[11] toward her. He was clearly unhappy, and she doubted[12] whether he still loved her. She could see he was confused.

The next day, while having tea, Marianne noticed a ring on Edward's finger.

"I've never seen that before, Edward. Is that your sister's hair in the ring?"

Edward blushed[13] deeply and, looking quickly at Elinor, answered, "Yes, it's Fanny's hair. It looks lighter than it really is."

Elinor was sure that he had taken some of her hair without her knowing.

Check Up

How does Marianne imagine her life with Willoughby?

a In a huge mansion with many servants

b In a small cottage in the countryside with no servants

c anywhere with a few servants, horses, and a carriage

Ans: c

Understanding the Story

Reason vs. Emotion

The very title of "Sense and Sensibility" refers to[1] the main theme of contrasting[2] styles found not only in the book but also in society at the time the novel was written. The two main characters, Elinor and Marianne, symbolize these two contrasts. Each woman behaves toward her respective[3] love very differently. On one hand, Elinor merely expresses "concern[4]" for her love, Edward Ferrars, while hiding her true feelings. On the other hand, Marianne shamelessly and passionately expresses her infatuation[5] with John Willoughby.

These contrasting styles reflect[6] the difference between "sense" and "sensibility." "Sense," of course, refers to "common sense": doing things in a practical and rational[7] manner[8]. "Sensibility", in its most common definition, refers to being able to feel or respond emotionally to something.

1. **refer to** 參考；與……有關聯
2. **contrast** [`kɑːntræst] (v.) 使……有對比
3. **respective** [rɪ`spektɪv] (a.) 分別的；各自的
4. **concern** [kən`sɜːrn] (n.) 關心；在乎
5. **infatuation** [ɪnˏfætʃu`eɪʃən] (n.) 迷戀
6. **reflect** [rɪ`flekt] (v.) 反映出

In portraying these opposite types of behavior, Austen may have been influenced by the social changes of the time. The cultural movement known as Classicism[9], closely associated with the Enlightenment, was coming to an end. Elinor represented this style of thinking and behavior. Romanticism was on the rise, and this movement is well represented in the actions of Marianne. However, Austen did not intend merely contrast to the differences between these two styles in rigid[10] characters. Elinor is also passionate, and Marianne becomes more rational at the end of the story. Perhaps Austen wanted the readers to ponder the best and worst qualities of each, while acknowledging[11] that we all contain[12] elements[13] of each.

7. **rational** [ˋræʃənəl] (a.) 理智的
8. **manner** [ˋmænər] (n.) 方法；方式
9. **Classicism** [ˋklæsɪsɪzəm] (n.) 古典主義
10. **rigid** [ˋrɪdʒɪd] (a.) 精確的；死板的
11. **acknowledge** [əkˋnɑːlɪdʒ] (v.) 承認
12. **contain** [kənˋteɪn] (v.) 包含
13. **element** [ˋelɪmənt] (n.) 元素；要素

Secrets

19

Sir John soon had more visitors at Barton Park. He had recently met two young ladies with the family name Steele, who were his distant cousins. He had invited them to visit, and they had accepted immediately.

The Dashwood sisters came to Barton Park to meet Sir John's new guests. They found the Steele sisters polite and elegant[1]. The elder sister Anne looked very plain[2], but the younger sister Lucy was a beautiful twenty-three-year-old lady.

"Miss Dashwood," asked the elder Miss Steele, "do you like Devonshire? You must've been sorry[3] to leave beautiful Norland."

---

1. **elegant** [ˋelɪgənt] (a.) 漂亮的；優雅的
2. **plain** [pleɪn] (a.) 樸素的；普通的
3. **sorry** [ˋsɔːri] (a.) 感到難過的；感到遺憾的
4. **lovely** [ˋlʌvli] (a.) 可愛的；動人的
5. **Good Heavens** 天啊
6. **vulgar** [ˋvʌlgər] (a.) 庸俗的
7. **clever** [ˋklevər] (a.) 小聰明的；機巧的

Elinor was surprised that the Steeles knew about her family. "Yes, Norland is a lovely[4] place."

"You must've had many handsome bachelors there," added Anne.

"Good Heavens[5], Anne," cried Lucy, "all you think and talk about is men!"

Elinor was glad when their meeting was finished. She found the elder Steele sister's conversation too vulgar[6] and the younger sister Lucy too clever[7] for her taste. The Steeles thought differently, and soon the young ladies were together for an hour or two every day.

One Point Lesson

- You **must've been** sorry to leave beautiful Norland.
  離開美麗的北國莊園，你一定很難過。

must have ＋過去分詞：一定有……（表過去有做的事）

e.g. He **must have robbed** the bank.
他一定是搶了銀行了。

20

Sir John told the Steeles everything about the Dashwoods' lives. One day, Anne Steele congratulated Elinor on Marianne's engagement to a very fine young man. Then the Steeles told Elinor that Sir John talked about her suspected[1] attachment to Edward.

"His name is Ferrars," whispered Sir John. "But it's a big secret!"

"Mr. Ferrars!" repeated Anne Steele, "Your sister-in-law's brother? He's a very pleasant[2] young man. We know him well."

"How can you say that, Anne?" cried Lucy, who always corrected everything her sister said. "We've only seen him once or twice at my uncle's house."

Elinor was shocked. She wanted to know who their uncle was and how they knew Edward. But she didn't ask questions.

During the next few days, Lucy took every chance to make conversation with Elinor.

---

1. **suspected** [sə`spektɪd] (a.) 有嫌疑的；可能存在的
2. **pleasant** [`plezənt] (a.) 令人愉快的；討人喜歡的
3. **insincerity** [ˏɪnsɪn`serəti] (n.) 不誠懇
4. **dishonesty** [dɪs`ɑːnɪsti] (n.) 不正直
5. **self-interest** [self `ɪntrɪst] (n.) 利己主義；私利
6. **lie behind** 隱藏在後 (lie-lay-lain)

She was a clever and humorous companion, but Elinor pitied her for lacking education. She disliked the insincerity[3], dishonesty[4], and self-interest[5] that lay behind[6] her words and actions.

While Elinor and Lucy were walking alone, Lucy asked, "You may think this question strange, but do you know your sister-in-law's mother, Mrs. Ferrars?"

Check Up

What does Elinor think of Lucy?

a Lucy is a trustworthy person.

b Lucy is very wise and well-educated.

c Lucy is not a nice person.

Ans: c

21

The question was strange to Elinor. "I've never met her," she answered coldly.

"Then, you couldn't say what kind of woman she is?" questioned Lucy.

"No," Elinor plainly[1] replied, holding back her true opinion of Edward's mother. "I don't know anything about her."

Then Lucy looked at Elinor. "I wish I could tell you about the difficult situation I'm in!"

"Well, I wish I could help you, but I don't know Mrs. Ferrars."

"Mrs. Ferrars knows nothing of me," Lucy said with a shy, sidelong[2] glance[3] at Elinor, "but we will be closely[4] connected soon."

"Good Lord!" cried Elinor, "Do you mean with Mr. Robert Ferrars?"

1. **plainly** [ˋpleɪnli] (adv.) 平淡地；明顯地
2. **sidelong** [ˋsaɪdlɒːŋ] (a.) 橫向的
3. **glance** [glæns] (n.) 瞥見
4. **closely** [ˋklousli] (adv.) 緊密地
5. **look upon *A* as *B*** 將 A 視為 B
6. **force oneself to** 強迫自己……

She didn't like the idea of Lucy becoming her sister-in-law.

"No," replied Lucy, "not Robert. I've never met him in my life. I mean his elder brother, Edward."

Elinor was silent with shock.

"You must be surprised," said Lucy, "because he never mentioned our relationship to your family. I know Edward won't be angry that I've told you our secret. He trusts you so much and looks upon you and your family almost as[5] sisters."

Elinor forced herself to[6] remain calm. "May I ask how long you have been engaged?"

"We've been engaged for four years now," she answered.

Elinor couldn't believe it.

22

"We met here in Devonshire while Edward was studying law," said Lucy. "I didn't want to get engaged without his mother's approval[1]. But I was young and loved him so much. Oh, dear Edward. Look, I carry his picture everywhere."

She pulled a small painting of Edward from her pocket and showed it to Elinor. Her heart sank[2].

"You can't imagine my suffering[3]," continued Lucy. "We see each other so infrequently[4]."

She put her hand to her eyes. Elinor was unsympathetic[5].

"Sometimes I think about breaking it off[6]," continued Lucy. "But I couldn't bear[7] hurting him. What do you think?"

1. **approval** [ə`pru:vəl] (n.) 同意
2. **sink** [sɪŋk] (v.) 下沉
3. **suffering** [`sʌfərɪŋ] (n.) 受苦
4. **infrequently** [ɪn`fri:kwəntli] (adv.) 不常地
5. **unsympathetic** [ˌʌnsɪmpə`θetɪk] (a.) 冷漠的
6. **break off** 停止；中斷
7. **bear** [ber] (v.) 忍受
8. **for oneself** 為自己

"You must decide for yourself[8]," answered Elinor.

"Poor Edward doesn't even have my picture," Lucy went on[9], "but I sent him a ring with a lock of my hair in it. Did you see him wearing it when he visited you recently?"

"I did," Elinor answered. Her calm voice concealed[10] her great unhappiness. She was shocked, confused, and miserable.

Their conversation ended, and Elinor was sure Edward still cared for her. She felt he loved her and would never have intentionally[11] deceived[12] her. He was trapped by a beautiful yet insincere[13], vulgar, selfish girl. Her interest lay in his future income[14].

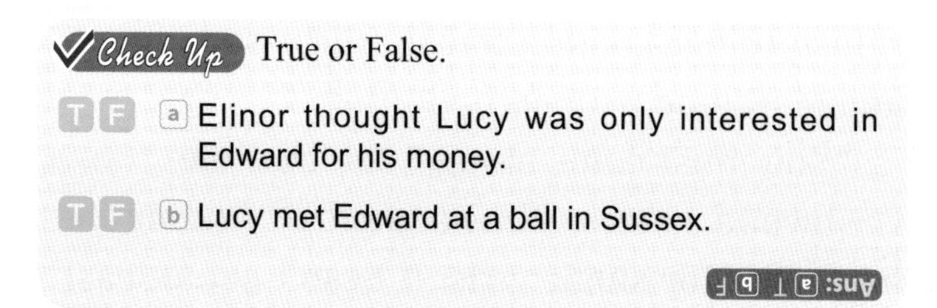

9. **go on** 繼續
10. **conceal** [kən`siːl] (v.) 隱瞞
11. **intentionally** [ɪn`tenʃənəli] (adv.) 故意地；存心地
12. **deceive** [dɪ`siːv] (v.) 欺騙
13. **insincere** [ˌɪnsɪn`sɪər] (a.) 不誠實的
14. **income** [`ɪŋkʌm] (n.) 收入

23

Elinor was very careful to hide her unhappiness. She knew if she told her family the bad news about Edward, their misery would only add to her own.

On several occasions[1], she spoke quietly with Lucy about the situation. Elinor learned that Lucy planned to hold Edward to[2] the engagement. She was jealous that Edward held Elinor in such high esteem[3]. Why else would Lucy tell Elinor her secret, but to warn her to keep away from[4] Edward?

What made Elinor most sad was that she knew Edward did not love his future wife. He had no chance of having a happy marriage.

Mrs. Jennings, who was making plans to return to her London house, surprised Elinor and Marianne with an invitation.

"You must come along," she told the Dashwood sisters, "I'm so good at[5] finding husbands for single girls. If I can't get at least[6] one of you married, it won't be my fault[7] !"

---

1. **occasion** [əˋkeɪʒən] (n.) 場合
2. **hold *A* to** 約束 A
3. **hold *A* in high esteem** 極為尊重（珍惜）A
4. **keep away from** 遠離……
5. **be good at** 擅長於
6. **at least** 至少
7. **fault** [fɔːlt] (n.) 過錯
8. **run into** 遇見

Elinor wanted to refuse. She feared she might run into[8] Edward and Lucy Steele in London. But Marianne was excited at the chance of seeing Willoughby who was still in London. Mrs. Dashwood insisted that they accept the invitation.

Check Up

Why was Elinor reluctant to tell her family about Lucy and Edward?

a She didn't want to make them sad.
b She promised Lucy she wouldn't tell anyone.
c She didn't want to make Lucy embarrassed.

Ans: a

24

When Elinor and Marianne got to[1] their room in Mrs. Jennings' luxurious[2] house in London, both girls took out[3] their pens and paper for letter writing.

"I'm writing home to Mother," said Elinor to Marianne. "Perhaps you should hold off[4] a few days."

"I'm not writing to Mother," replied Marianne.

---

1. **get to** 到達
2. **luxurious** [lʌg`ʒuriəs] (a.) 豪華的；奢華的
3. **take out** 拿出
4. **hold off** 推遲
5. **anxiously** [`æŋkʃəslɪ] (adv.) 焦慮地
6. **calmness** [`kɑːlmnɪs] (n.) 平靜
7. **bitter** [`bɪtər] (a.) 苦楚的

Elinor realized her sister was writing to Willoughby. Marianne was nervous for the rest of the evening. She could eat almost nothing, and anxiously[5] listened to the sound of every passing carriage. After dinner, there was a knock on the door. Marianne jumped up and cried, "It must be Willoughby!"

She ran toward the door and almost threw herself into the arms of Colonel Brandon. Her shock was too great to bear with calmness[6]. She left the room, and Elinor greeted the colonel. Elinor was sorry to see the man so in love with her sister. He experienced only her bitter[7] disappointment when she saw him.

The colonel asked, "Is she ill?"

Elinor made several excuses[8] about tiredness[9] and headaches[10]. Mrs. Jennings entered the room cheerfully and asked the colonel where he had been.

The colonel replied politely but gave no definitive[11] answer. He soon left, and all of the ladies went to bed early.

---

8. **make an excuse** 編造藉口
9. **tiredness** [`taɪrdnɪs] (n.) 疲倦
10. **headache** [`hedeɪk] (n.) 頭痛
11. **definitive** [dɪ`fɪnɪtɪv] (a.) 確定的；確切的

25

The next day found Marianne cheerfully hoping to see Willoughby. She was terribly distracted[1] all day. When the ladies returned from shopping, there was still no answer from Willoughby. After being at Mrs. Jennings' house for a week, Marianne finally saw Willoughby's card on the table when they came home from a ride.

"He's been here while we were out," exclaimed Marianne. From then on[2], she stayed at home while the others went out.

When a letter came the next day, Marianne tried to grab[3] it. But it was for Mrs. Jennings.

"Were you expecting a letter?" asked Elinor, who could see her sister's disappointment.

"Just a little," sighed Marianne.

"Dear sister, don't you trust me?" asked Elinor.

"How can you, who trusts in no one, ask me that?" replied Marianne.

---

1. **distracted** [dɪˋstræktɪd] (a.) 分心的
2. **from then on** 從那時開始
3. **grab** [græb] (v.) 抓
4. **bluster** [ˋblʌstər] (v.) 咆嘯地說
5. **reveal** [rɪˋviːl] (v.) 展現；揭露
6. **communicate** [kəˋmjuːnɪkeɪt] (v.) 傳達
7. **festivity** [feˋstɪvɪty] (n.) 宴會

"I have nothing to tell," Elinor blustered[4], wanting to reveal[5] the secret of Lucy Steele's engagement to Edward.

"Nor do I," replied Marianne. "You communicate[6] nothing, and I hide nothing."

The next day, there was a dance at Lady Middleton's London home. When Marianne realized Willoughby wasn't there, she lost interest in the festivities[7]. She was hurt that Willoughby was invited but hadn't come.

One night, the two Dashwood sisters went to a party with Lady Middleton. Willoughby was there, standing with an elegant young lady. Marianne was delighted when she saw him. She began to run to him, but Elinor stopped[1] her.

"Be calm," said Elinor. "Hide your feelings."

It was impossible for Marianne. She sat with anxiety[1] and impatience[2] written on her face.

"Why won't he look at me?" cried Marianne.

Finally, Willoughby turned around and looked at them. Marianne jumped up and held her hand out[3] to him. He came over and spoke to Elinor, not Marianne, asking about their mother's health.

Marianne blushed and cried, "Willoughby, why didn't you visit me?"

"I visited," he said, "but you weren't home."

"Haven't you received my letters?" she said with wild anxiety. "There must have been some terrible mistake. I beg you to tell me. What's the matter?"

Willoughby looked ashamed[4], glancing over at the young lady he had been standing next to earlier.

"Yes, I received the information that you were in town. Thank you for it."

With that, he turned away to join a friend.

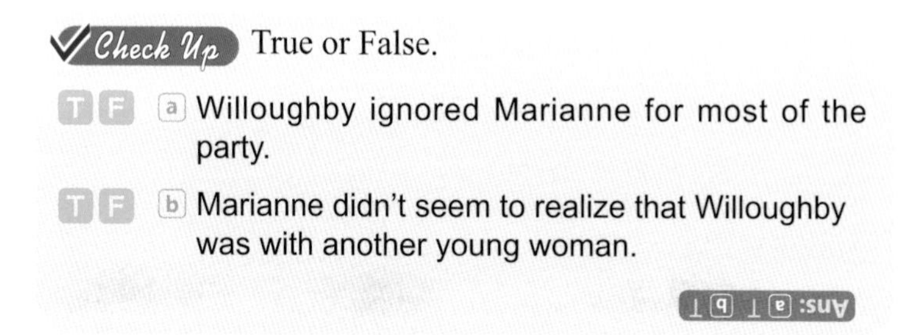

1. **anxiety** [æŋ`zaɪəti] (n.) 焦慮
2. **impatience** [ɪm`peɪʃəns] (n.) 不耐煩
3. **hold out** 給予
4. **ashamed** [ə`ʃeɪmd] (a.) 慚愧的

27

Marianne was pale[1] and unable to stand. Elinor helped her into a chair. Willoughby left the party soon after. Riding home, Elinor realized that Marianne's attachment with Willoughby was over[2]. She felt bitter over his tasteless[3] manner of ending it.

That night, Elinor was kept awake by the sound of Marianne sobbing. The next day, a letter arrived for Marianne. Mrs. Jennings asked if it was a love letter. "I've never seen a woman so in love in my life. I hope he won't keep her waiting."

When Elinor went into their room, Marianne was sobbing violently[4]. Elinor held her hand and burst into tears, too. Then she read his letter.

1. **pale** [peɪl] (a.) 蒼白的
2. **be over** 結束
3. **tasteless** [ˋteɪstləs] (a.) 無品味的；無禮的
4. **violently** [ˋvaɪələntli] (adv.) 猛烈地
5. **forgiveness** [fərˋgɪvnɪs] (n.) 諒解
6. **fondness** [ˋfɑːndnɪs] (n.) 喜愛
7. **impression** [ɪmˋpreʃən] (n.) 印象；感想

Dear Madam,

I beg your forgiveness[5] *if you didn't approve of my behavior last night. I will always remember our visits with great fondness*[6]*. I hope I didn't give you the impression*[7] *that I felt more for you than I ever expressed. Please understand that I've been engaged to someone else for a long time. We will be married soon. With this letter, I am returning the lock of your hair that you so kindly offered me.*

Your friend,
John Willoughby

Check Up

What is the tone of the letter Willoughby sent to Marianne?

a Cold and formal
b Formal and promising
c Generous and passionate

Ans: a

28

Elinor was disgusted[1] with the cold, official[2] manner of this letter. It was hurtful[3] and cruel. In an instant[4], she was glad that Marianne would not wed[5] such a terrible man.

"Oh, Elinor," said Marianne, "I'm sorry to make you so unhappy."

"Just think how much you would have suffered[6] if you'd discovered how terrible he was at the end of your engagement," replied Elinor.

"Engagement!" cried Marianne. "We were never engaged. He never promised me anything."

"He said he loved you?" questioned Elinor.

"No, he never said so," cried Marianne. "But I could feel it in his eyes."

She began sobbing again.

1. **disgusted** [dɪs`gʌstɪd] (a.) 感到作嘔的
2. **official** [ə`fɪʃəl] (a.) 制式化的；官腔的
3. **hurtful** [`hɜ:rtfəl] (a.) 傷人的
4. **in an instant** 一剎那
5. **wed** [wed] (v.) 結婚
6. **suffer** [`sʌfər] (v.) 受苦
7. **concern** [kən`sɜ:n] (n.) 關心
8. **spend *A* on *B*** 花 A 在 B 上
9. **badly** [`bædli] (adv.) 非常
10. **all for the best** 一勞永逸

Later, Mrs. Jennings showed concern[7] for Marianne, who had made herself sick. She told them that Willoughby's other woman was Miss Grey, with an income of 50,000 pounds per year and that Willoughby spent too much money on[8] his carriage and horses and needed money very badly[9]. She thought his behavior was terrible. But cheerfully she said that it was all for the best[10] because now Marianne could marry Colonel Brandon.

Comprehension Quiz Chapters Two & Three

A Fill in the blanks with proper words.

intentionally vulgar company calm bachelors

1. Willoughby openly enjoyed Marianne's ___________.
2. You must've had many handsome ___________ there.
3. She found the elder Steele sister's conversation too ___________.
4. Elinor forced herself to remain ___________.
5. She felt he never would have _______________ deceived her.

B Choose the correct usage.

1. (a) They were delighted at the blue sky and the white clouds.
   (b) Willoughby were delighted for a rude entrance.
2. (a) Colonel Brandon was imagined about Marianne.
   (b) She imagined her hero so intensely that she didn't notice the pain.
3. (a) Willoughby possessed the sensibility that Edward Ferrars lacked.
   (b) Marianne fell down the hill and lacked her ankle.

C Choose the correct answer.

1 What did Mrs. Dashwood and Elinor do when a stranger carried Marianne into the house?

(a) They called the police.

(b) They shot him with a gun.

(c) They noticed his handsome appearance.

2 Why did Willoughby want to marry Miss Grey?

(a) Because she was the most beautiful woman in England.

(b) Because she was rich, and he badly needed money.

(c) Because she was more intelligent than Marianne.

D Rearrange the following sentences in chronological order.

1 Colonel Brandon received a letter.

2 The group tried to persuade Colonel Brandon to put his business off.

3 The group planned to go on a trip to a country house.

4 Colonel Brandon said he had to leave on urgent business.

5 Marianne got into Willoughby's carriage and disappeared for the rest of the day.

______ ⇨ ______ ⇨ ______ ⇨ ______ ⇨ ______

29 The Truth Revealed

Marianne felt more miserable the next day. She was determined to[1] avoid Mrs. Jennings.

"Her kindness is not sympathy[2]," she complained. "She enjoys gossiping[3] about my problems to her friends."

After breakfast, Mrs. Jennings found the sisters in their room and delivered[4] a letter to Marianne. "My dear, this will make you happy."

Marianne hoped it was from Willoughby, explaining and apologizing for his strange behavior. But it was from her mother. The letter expressed confidence in Willoughby. Marianne began to cry again at the thought of her mother's disappointment when she learned the truth about him.

Then there was a knock on the door. It was Colonel Brandon. Marianne ran away to her room. Elinor greeted him. He seemed unhappy.

"I've come to speak with you," Brandon said to Elinor. "I want to tell you some details about Mr. Willoughby's character[5]."

"Your words are proof[6] of your feelings for Marianne," said Elinor.

"Perhaps you remember a lady I mentioned once at Barton Park? She was like your sister, with an eager[7] mind, a warm heart, and great sensibility. She was a distant cousin of mine. We played together when we were children, and this grew into love," said Brandon.

1. **be determined to**
   下定決心要……
2. **sympathy** [`sɪmpəθi] (n.)
   同情；認同
3. **gossip** [`gɑːsəp] (v.)
   八卦；說人閒話
4. **deliver** [dɪ`lɪvər] (v.) 傳送
5. **character** [`kærɪktər] (n.)
   個性；人品
6. **proof** [pruːf] (n.) 證據
7. **eager** [`iːgər] (a.)
   熱心的；急切的

30

"But at seventeen, she was married to my brother against her wishes. Before the wedding, we planned to run away to marry secretly. My father discovered the plan and sent me to the army[1]. Their marriage was unhappy. My brother cheated on[2] her with countless[3] other women. Two years later, they were divorced[4]."

Elinor looked upon[5] him with great sympathy and concern.

1. **army** [`ɑːrmi] (n.) 軍隊
2. **cheat on** 欺騙；背叛
3. **countless** [`kaʊntləs] (a.) 數不清的
4. **be divorced** 離婚
5. **look upon** 看待
6. **debtor** [`detər] (n.) 債務人
7. **respectable** [rɪ`spektəbəl] (a.) 可敬的

He continued, "Three years later, I found her in a debtor's[6] prison. She was terribly sick and had only a short while left to live. I cared for her until she died in my arms. She left a little girl in my care named Eliza. I sent Eliza to school and then left her in the care of a respectable[7] woman in the country. Eliza is now seventeen. Last year, she suddenly disappeared[8]. She was gone for eight months, while I searched for[9] her."

"Good Lord!" cried Elinor. "Could Willoughby be . . ."

"Remember the day at Barton Park? We were supposed to[10] go on the outing[11], but I received an urgent letter. I was called away[12]. Willoughby didn't know it was to help someone he'd made poor and miserable. But he wouldn't have cared. He did the worst a man could do. He left a girl he'd seduced[13], with no home, no friends, and no money."

8. **disappear** [ˌdɪsəˋpɪr] (v.) 消失
9. **search for** 尋找
10. **be supposed to** 應該要
11. **outing** [ˋaʊtɪŋ] (n.) 遠足；郊遊
12. **call away** 轉移；叫走
13. **seduce** [siˋdjuːs] (v.) 誘拐；誘姦

"This is an outrage[1]" cried Elinor.

"Now you understand what he is like. Imagine how hard it was for me to see your sister's affection for him when I knew of his character. Who knows what his intentions were toward her? One day she will feel grateful[2] when she compares her situation to[3] that of my poor Eliza."

"Have you seen Willoughby since you left Barton?" asked Elinor.

"Yes, after Eliza confessed[4] the name of her seducer[5]. I accused him of dishonorable[6] behavior and challenged him to a duel[7]. We met in combat[8], but both of us returned

---

1. **outrage** [ˋautreɪdʒ] (n.) 惡行；嚴重的不法行為
2. **grateful** [ˋgreɪtfəl] (a.) 感激的
3. **compare *A* to *B*** 比較 A 與 B
4. **confess** [kənˋfes] (v.) 坦白；承認
5. **seducer** [siˋdjuːsər] (n.) 玩弄女性的人；騙子
6. **dishonorable** [dɪsˋɑːnərəbəl] (a.) 可恥的；卑鄙的
7. **challenge *A* to a duel** 與 A 決鬥
8. **combat** [ˋkɑːmbæt] (n.) 打鬥
9. **unwounded** [ʌnˋwuːndɪd] (a.) 未受傷的
10. **result** [rɪˋzʌlt] (n.) 結果

unwounded[9]. My poor Eliza had her child and now lives in the country."

The colonel left. Elinor told her sister the details of their conversation. But the result[10] was not what she had hoped. Marianne listened attentively and accepted Willoughby's guilt[11]. But she seemed even more saddened[12] that Willoughby's good character was lost, as well as his heart.

Mrs. Dashwood's letter of reply[13] came the following day. She advised them not to[14] shorten[15] their stay with Mrs. Jennings. A hasty[16] return to Barton would only bring back memories of happy times with Willoughby.

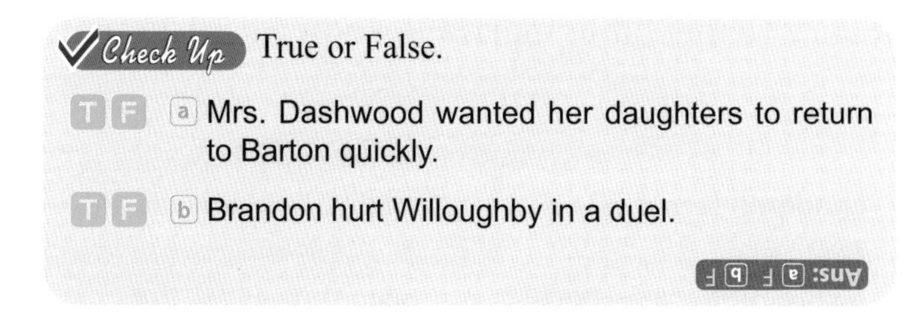

11. **guilt** [gɪlt] (n.) 犯罪；過失
12. **sadden** [`sædn] (v.) 悲痛
13. **reply** [rɪ`plaɪ] (n.) 回應
14. **advise *A* to** 建議 A……
15. **shorten** [`ʃɔːrtən] (v.) 縮短
16. **hasty** [`heɪsti] (a.) 倉促的；急忙的

Sir John and Mrs. Jennings condemned[1] Willoughby when they heard of his dishonor[2]. They also shared the belief[3] that Elinor would be the woman to marry Colonel Brandon.

Two weeks after Willoughby's letter, Elinor found out that he had gotten married. Marianne was calm when she first received the news, but later began to sob wildly[4].

At this time, Elinor unhappily met the Steele sisters who had arrived in London. Lucy pretended to be happy to meet her. Elinor had to use all of her self-control to remain polite.

A more welcome meeting occurred[5] when John Dashwood visited them at Mrs. Jennings'. After being introduced[6] to Colonel Brandon, he asked Elinor to take a walk with him privately. "Elinor, I think I'll be congratulating you on a very respectable marriage soon," said John.

1. **condemn** [kən`dem] (v.) 譴責
2. **dishonor** [dɪs`ɑːnər] (n.) 丟臉；不名譽
3. **belief** [bɪ`liːf] (n.) 相信
4. **wildly** [`waɪldli] (adv.) 失去控制地
5. **occur** [ə`kɜːr] (v.) 發生
6. **introduce** [ɪntrə`djuːs] (v.) 介紹
7. **at the same time** 同時間

"Colonel Brandon is most gentlemanly, and I'm sure he likes you."

"He doesn't wish to marry me," she replied.

"You're wrong, Sister. You can catch him with a little effort. How funny it would be if Fanny had a brother and I had a sister, marrying at the same time[7]!"

"Is Mr. Edward Ferrars getting married?" Elinor asked calmly.

Check Up

Why did John think Colonel Brandon was in love with Elinor?

a John noticed how Colonel Brandon acted toward Elinor.
b Colonel Brandon told John he loved Elinor.
c Mrs. Dashwood told John's wife Brandon loved Elinor.

Ans: a

33

"It's not arranged[1] yet. But he is to wed the lady Miss Morton. She's Lord Morton's only daughter, with 30,000 pounds of her own. Edward's mother will give him 1,000 pounds per year if he marries her. I wish we could be so comfortable," he said.

A week later, John and Fanny Dashwood gave a dinner party. The Middletons, Mrs. Jennings, Colonel Brandon, the Dashwood sisters, and the Steele sisters were all invited. Elinor and Lucy both knew that Mrs. Ferrars would be there.

"Oh dear, Miss Dashwood," whispered Lucy as they walked upstairs. "In a moment, I'll be seeing the person on whom my happiness depends – my future mother-in-law!"

Mrs. Ferrars was a small, scrawny[2] woman with a grouchy[3] expression. She clearly disliked Elinor and approved of Lucy Steele.

"If only[4] she knew Lucy's secret," mused[5] Elinor, "how she would hate her!"

---

1. **arrange** [ə`reɪndʒ] (v.) 安排
2. **scrawny** [`skrɔːni] (a.) 骨瘦如柴的
3. **grouchy** [`grautʃi] (a.) 愛抱怨的；不悅的
4. **if only** 但願；只要
5. **muse** [mjuːz] (v.) 沉思
6. **awkward** [`ɔːkwərd] (a.) 尷尬的
7. **keep watch over** 監視；緊盯著

The next morning, Lucy bragged to Elinor about how much Mrs. Ferrars liked her.

Before Elinor could reply, the door opened. Edward walked in. It was an awkward[6] moment between the three of them. Elinor welcomed him. Lucy kept watch over[7] Elinor from the corner of her eye. Elinor decided to leave the couple alone and went to find Marianne.

One Point Lesson

But he **is to** wed the lady Miss Morton.
他將會娶摩頓小姐。

be to ：將要……

e.g. You **are to** submit your paper by tomorrow.
你明天要將作業交出。

After visiting with his sisters, John Dashwood thought about inviting them to visit Norland for a few days. But Fanny Dashwood quickly informed him, "I'm shocked by your suggestion. I've just decided to ask the Steele sisters to stay with us. We'll have to ask your sisters some other year."

John agreed, and Fanny invited Lucy and her sister. Lucy was very happy for the useful opportunity[1] to be close to Edward.

1. **opportunity** [ˌɑːpər`tuːnəti] (n.) 機會
2. **creature** [`kriːtʃər] (n.) 生物；傢伙
3. **scream** [skriːm] (v.) 尖叫
4. **stand** [stænd] (v.) 忍受
5. **in preparation** 準備好

Some days later, Mrs. Jennings came back from her daughter Mrs. Palmer's house with a new piece of gossip.

"Fanny is ill because her brother Edward has been engaged to Lucy Steele for over a year! Only her sister Anne knew! The Steeles are staying at your brother's house right now. Anne, being a creature[2] of no intelligence, told Fanny! Your sister-in-law fell on the floor sobbing and screaming[3]. The Steele girls were told to pack their bags immediately. The Ferrars family wanted Edward to marry that rich Miss Morton. I have no pity for them. I can't stand[4] people who think money and greatness is important!"

Now all of the talk was about Edward. Elinor knew Marianne would be angry with him. She decided to tell her sister the truth in preparation[5].

Check Up Fill in the blank with correct word.

Mrs. Jennings learned a new piece of ___________, which she promptly told everyone she knew.

Ans: gossip

35

Marianne listened to Elinor's story in horror[1] and cried continuously[2]. Edward seemed like a second Willoughby.

"How long have you known?" she asked.

"Lucy told me of her engagement four months ago at Barton. I promised to keep it a secret[3]."

"All this time you've been caring for me, and you've had this on your heart. How could you put up with[4] it?" cried Marianne.

---

1. **in horror** 震驚地
2. **continuously** [kən`tɪnjuəsli] (adv.) 連續地
3. **keep *A* a secret** 保守秘密
4. **put up with** 忍受
5. **duty** [`du:ti] (n.) 責任；義務
6. **ill will** 惡意；敵意
7. **on one's mind** 在心上
8. **destroy** [dɪ`strɔɪ] (v.) 摧毀
9. **defeat** [dɪ`fi:t] (v.) 打敗
10. **endure** [ɪn`dʊr] (v.) 忍受
11. **rudeness** [`ru:dnɪs] (n.) 無禮

"I was just doing my duty[5]. I didn't want to worry everyone," replied Elinor.

"Four months! And yet you loved him!"

"Yes, but I love my family, too. And I don't have any ill will[6] toward Edward. They will marry, and in time he will forget that he ever thought another woman better than her."

"I'm beginning to understand the way you think. Your self-control doesn't seem so strange any more."

"I know you think I lack emotions. This has been on my mind[7] for months. I couldn't tell anyone. The person who destroyed[8] my hopes of happiness told me this. She saw me as a rival and was happy to defeat[9] me. I've had to listen to her talking about Edward again and again and pretend I wasn't interested in him. And I had to endure[10] the unkindness and rudeness[11] of his mother. Surely you can see how I've suffered now?"

One Point Lesson

Edward **seemed like** a second Willoughby.
愛德華簡直就是第二個威洛比。

seem + adj. / seem like + n.：就像是

e.g. He **seems** rich. / He **seems like** a rich man.
他看起來很有錢。/ 他看起來像個有錢人。

36

"Oh, Elinor!" Marianne cried. "How unkind I've been to you!"

Then the two sisters fell into each other's arms, sobbing.

The next day, John Dashwood came to visit them.

"I suppose[1] you've heard of our shocking discovery," he said.

The sisters nodded[2] silently.

"Your sister-in-law has suffered terribly. So has Mrs. Ferrars. They were both deceived. And after we showed those young women such kindness! Fanny wishes she'd invited you two to visit instead. Poor Mrs. Ferrars sent for[3] Edward, and he came to see her. I'm sorry to say what happened next. Our efforts to persuade Edward to end his engagement were useless[4].

---

1. **suppose** [sə`poʊz] (v.) 猜想
2. **nod** [nɑːd] (v.) 點頭
3. **send for** 派人去叫
4. **useless** [`juːsləs] (a.) 無用處的；無效的
5. **offer to** 主動提議
6. **do one's best** 盡其所能
7. **prevent *A* from** 使 A 無法……
8. **succeed in** 成功於……
9. **understandable** [ˌʌndər`stændəbəl] (a.) 可理解的
10. **stubbornness** [`stʌbərnɪs] (n.) 頑固
11. **astonishing** [ə`stɑːnɪʃɪŋ] (a.) 驚人的

His mother offered to[5] give him 1,000 pounds per year to marry Miss Morton. But he refused. Mrs. Ferrars told him he would receive no money from her, and she would do her best[6] to prevent him from[7] succeeding in[8] any profession he entered."

"Good Heavens!" cried Marianne. "It's so terrible!"

"Your shock is understandable[9]," John said to his sisters. "His stubbornness[10] is astonishing[11]."

Check Up True or False.

T F a Fanny now liked the Dashwood sisters more than the Steele sisters.

T F b Mrs. Ferrars has become Edward's enemy.

Ans: a F b T

37

"Mr. Ferrars has behaved like an honest man," cried Mrs. Jennings who was listening to them. "He must keep his promise[1] to marry Lucy Steele."

"Madam, I respect your opinion," replied John, "but a good woman like Mrs. Ferrars, with such an enormous[2] fortune, cannot approve of her son's secret engagement to an unsuitable[3] woman. Mrs. Ferrars told Edward to leave her house forever, and he did. She never wants to see him again. Robert shall inherit her fortune when she dies. Edward will be poor, while his younger brother is wealthy! I sincerely pity him."

John Dashwood soon left, and the three women condemned[4] Mrs. Ferrars' behavior and warmly supported Edward.

A letter from Lucy came the next morning.

---

1. **keep one's promise** 遵守承諾
2. **enormous** [ɪ`nɔːrməs] (a.) 巨大的；可觀的
3. **unsuitable** [ʌn`suːtəbəl] (a.) 不適合的
4. **condemn** [kən`dem] (v.) 譴責
5. **hope for the best** 往好地方想
6. **recommend** [ˏrekə`mend] (v.) 推薦
7. **send one's regards to** 表達關心

Dear Miss Dashwood,

As a true friend, I know you will be pleased to hear this. Despite the terrible suffering that Edward and I have been through, we are quite well now, thank God. We are happy in each other's love. Thank you for helping us through our difficulties. Yesterday, we spent two hours together, and I offered him his freedom, and was ready to call our engagement off if he desired. But he refused. He said he didn't care about his mother's anger as long as I loved him.

Life will not be easy for us, but we must hope for the best[5]*. He will enter the Church. I hope you can recommend*[6] *him to somebody who can offer him a job. Please tell dear Mrs. Jennings that I hope she won't forget us, either. Please remember me well and send my regards to*[7] *Sir John and Lady Middleton, their dear children, and give my love to Miss Marianne.*

Yours Truly,
Lucy Steele

38

Elinor was sure that Lucy wanted Mrs. Jennings to see the letter and showed it to her immediately. The old woman praised[1] Lucy's warm heart. "She calls me dear Mrs. Jennings! Oh, I wish I could get him a job with all my heart[2]!"

The Dashwood sisters had been in London for more than two months. Marianne was ready to go home. She missed the country terribly[3]. Elinor was also anxious to[4] go. But she dreaded[5] the long journey that lay ahead. This problem was solved when the Palmers invited Mrs. Jennings and the Dashwood sisters to their home in Somerset, only a day away from Barton.

They accepted the invitation and planned to stay at the Palmers' home for a week.

1. **praise** [preɪz] (v.) 讚賞
2. **with all one's heart** 全心全意地
3. **terribly** [`terɪbli] (adv.) 非常地
4. **be anxious to** 急切於……
5. **dread** [dred] (v.) 擔心；害怕
6. **minister** [`mɪnɪstər] (n.) 牧師；部長
7. **light** [laɪt] (a.) 輕的

A few days later, Colonel Brandon came to speak with Elinor. He had a job for Edward.

"It would be a start for Mr. Ferrars at least," continued Colonel Brandon. "The minister's[6] duties there are light[7], and a cottage comes with the job. I'm sorry for the smallness of the house, and the income is only 200 pounds a year."

Elinor thanked the colonel and promised to tell Edward the good news.

Understanding the Story

A Humble[1] Author

Jane Austen did not seek fame as an author. In fact, she avoided fame like the plague. This was not because she was shy or modest; rather, it was more because of the social constraints[2] placed on women in eighteenth century England.

Women who entered the public[3] arena[4] through work, politics, or art were negatively received by the public. These women were thought of as having lost their precious femininity[5]. As a result of this prejudice[6], Austen's name was not mentioned anywhere in the first and second editions. The first edition mysteriously[7] claimed the author was "a lady". In the second edition, authorship[8] was attributed to[9] "the author of *Pride and Prejudice*."

---

1. **humble** [ˋhʌmbəl] (a.) 謙遜的
2. **constraint** [kənˋstreɪnt] (n.) 約束；限制
3. **public** [ˋpʌblɪk] (a.) 公眾的
4. **arena** [əˋriːnə] (n.) 場域
5. **femininity** [ˏfemɪˋnɪnɪti] (n.) 女性氣質
6. **prejudice** [ˋpredʒədɪs] (n.) 偏見
7. **mysteriously** [mɪˋstɪriəsli] (adv.) 神祕地
8. **authorship** [ˋɑːθərʃɪp] (n.) 作者身分
9. **be attributed to** 出自

Austen feared the social repercussions[10] of being known as a writer so much that when she wrote at her home, she did so behind a door that creaked[11] when someone approached. Thus warned, Austen would quickly hide the manuscript she was working on and pretend to be doing something else.

Although this enabled Austen to maintain her private life and saved her from the harsh[12] and prejudiced spotlight, it is somewhat ironic that a woman responsible for throwing women's issues into the public eye would desire such an anonymous[13] lifestyle for herself. It is also a pity that Austen, who could have served as an exemplary[14] role model for other aspiring women writers, would choose to hide behind the conventions[15] of the society she so accurately portrayed and criticized. As a female author, she proved herself just as witty, insightful, and intelligent as other leading male authors of her day.

10. **repercussion** [ˌriːpəˋkʌʃən] (n.) 影響；後果
11. **creak** [kriːk] (v.) 發出咯吱聲
12. **harsh** [hɑːrʃ] (a.) 嚴厲的
13. **anonymous** [əˋnɑːnɪməs] (a.) 不具名的
14. **exemplary** [ɪgˋzempləri] (a.) 示範的
15. **convention** [kənˋvenʃəns] (n.) 常規；習俗

Chapter Five

Back to Barton

39

Before leaving London, Elinor visited her brother and Fanny. John was interested to hear of Colonel Brandon's job offer to Edward. John took her aside[1] and said, "I want to tell you one more thing. Although Mrs. Ferrars did not approve of Edward's attachment to you, she would have preferred he marry you than Lucy Steele. Of course, it's too late now."

1. **take *A* aside** 帶 A 到旁邊
2. **thoughtless** [`θɔːtləs] (a.) 粗心的；沒思想的
3. **self-important** [self ɪm`pɔːrtənt] (a.) 自大的

Suddenly, Robert Ferrars entered. She had only met the younger Ferrars brother once and found him to be a thoughtless[2] and self-important[3] young man. This meeting increased her dislike for him. He talked happily of how he would receive Edward's inheritance and laughed at the idea of Edward being a poor minister who lived in a cottage.

"I said to my mother," he said. "Dear madam, if Edward marries this young woman, I shall never see him again! If I'd known of this country girl earlier, I would have tried to persuade him to break it off!"

Elinor was glad she couldn't stay long and hoped she would never see Robert Ferrars again.

What did Robert Ferrars NOT do to make Elinor dislike him?

a He talked about how happy he was to get his brother's inheritance.

b He made fun of the idea of Edward being a poor minister.

c He told Elinor that she was not worthy of marrying his brother.

Ans: c

The trip to Cleveland, the Palmers' home in Somerset, took two days. When they arrived, Marianne felt worse than usual. They were only 30 miles away from Willoughby's country house. She planned to spend her time taking lonely walks and delighting in[1] her misery.

Colonel Brandon was also a guest of the Palmers. He spent a great deal of time talking to Elinor about the repairs[2] he would make to the minister's cottage at Delaford before Edward took up residence there. He talked to her so much that she began to wonder if John Dashwood had been right about the colonel's interest in her. But she still got the feeling that when Colonel Brandon spoke to her, he wished he was talking to Marianne.

1. **delight in** 以……為樂
2. **repair** [rɪ`per] (n.) 修理
3. **come down with** 染上……病
4. **feverish** [`fiːvərɪʃ] (a.) 發燒的
5. **soreness** [`sɔːrnɪs] (n.) 疼痛
6. **all over one's body** 全身上下
7. **infection** [ɪn`fekʃən] (n.) 傳染
8. **recover** [rɪ`kʌvər] (v.) 復元

After two evenings of walking in the thick wet grass, Marianne came down with[3] a terrible cold. She felt feverish[4], with soreness[5] all over her body[6]. She refused all medicine, insisting that all she needed was a good night's rest.

But by the next day, she was very sick. Elinor sent for the doctor, who said she suffered from an infection[7] and would recover[8] in a few days.

Check Up True or False.

T F ⓐ Marianne became sick after being bitten by an insect.

T F ⓑ Elinor realized that Colonel Brandon loved her.

Ans: ⓐ F ⓑ F

41

After several days, Marianne's condition remained the same. The doctor came every day. Elinor was hopeful[1] and in letters to her mother, didn't mention the seriousness[2] of Marianne's illness[3].

That evening, as Elinor sat beside her sister's bed, Marianne sat up suddenly and cried wildly, "Is Mama coming?"

1. **hopeful** [`houpfəl] (a.) 抱有希望的
2. **seriousness** [`sɪriənɪs] (n.) 嚴重
3. **illness** [`ɪlnɪs] (n.) 病痛
4. **lie down** 躺下
5. **desperately** [`despərɪtli] (adv.) 絕望地；極度地

"Not yet," Elinor replied, hiding her fear and helping Marianne lie down[4] again.

"Please tell her to come soon," Marianne cried desperately[5], "or I shall never see her again!"

Elinor was so alarmed that she sent for the doctor immediately. Colonel Brandon drove through the night to Barton to fetch[6] Mrs. Dashwood.

When the doctor came, he admitted[7] that the medicines had failed. The infection was stronger than ever. Elinor hoped her mother would arrive in time to say goodbye to her dying sister.

But by midday, signs[8] of Marianne's fever[9] were going down[10]. Elinor began to hope that Marianne would survive[11]. On the doctor's next visit, he congratulated her on Marianne's slow recovery[12]. That night, Elinor slept peacefully[13], knowing her sister was out of danger[14].

6. **fetch** [fetʃ] 去將……帶回
7. **admit** [əd`mɪt] (v.) 承認
8. **sign** [saɪn] (n.) 症狀；記號
9. **fever** [`fiːvər] (n.) 發燒
10. **go down** 下降
11. **survive** [sər`vaɪv] (v.) 存活
12. **recovery** [rɪ`kʌvəri] (n.) 復元
13. **peacefully** [`piːsfəli] (adv.) 平靜地
14. **out of danger** 脫離險境

42

Around eight o'clock, Elinor heard a carriage drive up to the front door[1]. She rushed downstairs to meet her mother. But in the sitting room she found Willoughby. Fearful[2], she stepped backward[3].

"Miss Dashwood, I have something to tell you," begged Willoughby.

Elinor agreed reluctantly[4], "Hurry, I have no spare[5] time."

"First of all[6], is your sister out of danger?"

"We hope so," Elinor replied frigidly[7].

"Thank God! I heard she was ill. I want to offer an explanation for my actions. I have not always been a scoundrel. I beg your sister's forgiveness."

"Marianne has already forgiven you."

1. **front door** 前門；入口處
2. **fearful** [ˋfɪrfəl] (a.) 害怕的；擔心的
3. **backward** [ˋbækwərd] (adv.) 向後地
4. **reluctantly** [rɪˋlʌktəntli] (a.) 不情願地
5. **spare** [sper] (a.) 空閒的
6. **first of all** 首先
7. **frigidly** [ˋfrɪdʒɪdli] (adv.) 冷淡地
8. **pass** [pæs] (v.) 度過
9. **debt** [det] (n.) 債務
10. **ask for a lady's hand** 求婚
11. **scandalous** [ˋskændələs] (a.) 醜聞的
12. **connection** [kəˋnekʃən] (n.) 關係

"Really?" he cried eagerly. "Still, I'll explain. When I first met her, my only intention was to pass[8] my time in Devonshire pleasantly. My debts[9] are great. I was planning to marry a woman of fortune. But I soon found myself falling in love with Marianne. By the time I'd prepared myself to ask for her hand[10] in marriage, my relative, old Mrs. Smith, discovered my scandalous[11] connection[12]," he blushed and turned away. "But you've probably heard that story from Colonel Brandon."

"I have," said Elinor who was also blushing.

Check Up Fill in the blank according to the story.

Willoughby claimed that he has not always been a __________.

Ans: scoundrel

43

Willoughby continued, "Mrs. Smith was very angry with me, and I suffered. She cut off[1] my money and refused to see me again. I knew that if I married Marianne, I would be poor. So I came to Barton Cottage to say goodbye. I was miserable when I saw her sorrow[2] and disappointment."

There was a short silence[3], and Elinor softened[4] toward him.

1. **cut off** 切斷
2. **sorrow** [ˋsɑːroʊ] (n.) 傷心
3. **silence** [ˋsaɪləns] (n.) 沉默
4. **soften** [ˋsɔːfən] (v.) 使和藹

"Marianne's notes to me were like knives in my heart. She was far dearer to me than Miss Grey, whom I was engaged to."

"Remember that you are a married man now," said Elinor.

Willoughby laughed wildly. "Married, yes. Miss Grey saw Marianne's last letter and was jealous and angry. As punishment[5], she made me write that terrible letter to Marianne."

"You have made your choice[6]," Elinor replied coldly. "Respect your wife."

"My wife doesn't deserve[7] your pity. I have no chance of happiness with her. If I'm ever free again. . ."

Elinor stopped him with a frown[8].

"I'll leave now," he said. "But I'll live in terror of[9] one event[10]. . . your sister's marriage."

"She can never be more lost to you than she is now," said Elinor.

"But she will be gained by someone else." With that, Willoughby ran away.

5. **punishment** [`pʌnɪʃmənt] (n.) 懲罰
6. **make one's choice** 做出選擇
7. **deserve** [dɪ`zɜːrv] (v.) 應得
8. **frown** [fraʊn] (n.) 皺眉
9. **in terror of** 懼怕
10. **event** [ɪ`vent] (n.) 事情

A half hour later, the girls' mother entered the house, half-dead with fear. Elinor gave her the good news. Mrs. Dashwood cried tears of relief[1]. Colonel Brandon shared their relief with his profound[2] silence.

Marianne's recovery continued daily. Mrs. Dashwood soon found an opportunity to tell Elinor other news. On the long drive from Barton, Colonel Brandon told Mrs. Dashwood he could no longer hide his feelings for Marianne. He would ask for her hand in marriage. Mrs. Dashwood, convinced of[3] his excellent character, hoped that in time, Marianne would accept his offer.

Marianne recovered quickly and returned to Barton in a week. On the ride home in Colonel Brandon's carriage, Elinor saw that Marianne was now able to control her feelings. Elinor was pleased to see her becoming enthusiastic[4] again.

---

1. **relief** [rɪ`li:f] (n.) 解除；緩和
2. **profound** [prə`faʊnd] (a.) 深度的
3. **convinced of** 對……確信的
4. **enthusiastic** [ɪn͵θu:zi`æstɪk] (a.) 熱情的
5. **impolite** [͵ɪmpə`laɪt] (a.) 無禮的
6. **broken heart** 碎裂的心
7. **take a deep breath** 深呼吸

A few days later, Marianne confessed to Elinor, "I behaved badly. I was too free with Willoughby and so impolite[5] to other people. I was terrible to you, dear Elinor. You were suffering, too. I thought only of my own broken heart[6]."

Elinor took a deep breath[7] and told Marianne everything Willoughby said to her. Marianne said nothing. Tears ran down her face.

Check Up

What did Colonel Brandon tell Mrs. Dashwood on the long drive from Barton?

a He told her that he wanted to ask for Elinor's hand in marriage.

b He said that he was in love with Marianne.

c He said that he could no longer lie about Willoughby.

Ans: b

45

That evening, Marianne told her mother and sister, "What Elinor told me was a great relief. I could have never been happy with him, knowing what he did."

"Happy with a scoundrel like that?" cried her mother. "Not my Marianne!"

"You're considering the matter like a sensible person," said Elinor.

"How foolish I was!" cried Marianne.

"It's all my fault," said Mrs. Dashwood. "I should have smelled his intentions earlier."

Life at Barton became normal again. Elinor waited for news of Edward. It arrived unexpectedly[1] from Mrs. Dashwood's manservant, Thomas. He returned with the report that "Mr. Ferrars was married."

Marianne took one look at[2] Elinor's pale face and burst into sobs. Mrs. Dashwood didn't know which daughter to comfort[3] first. She led Marianne to another room and hurried back to Elinor who had begun questioning Thomas. "Who told you this, Thomas?"

1. **unexpectedly** [ˌʌnɪkˋspektɪdli] (adv.) 意外地
2. **take a look at** 看了一眼
3. **comfort** [ˋkʌmfərt] (v.) 安慰
4. **former** [ˋfɔːrmər] (a.) 之前的

"I saw him myself, with the former[4] Miss Steele. She called to me from a carriage and asked about Marianne's health. Then she smiled and said her name had changed since she was last in Devonshire."

"Was Mr. Ferrars in the carriage with her?"

"Yes, Madam. He was next to her. But I didn't see his face."

One Point Lesson

I should have smelled his intentions earlier.
我早該嗅出他的不良意圖。

should have + 過去分詞：應該要……（實際上沒做到）

e.g. He **should have attended** the party.
他該參加派對的。

"Did Mrs. Ferrars look happy?" asked Elinor.

"Yes, Madam. Very happy indeed[1]."

Thomas was sent away while Elinor and her mother sat in silence. Mrs. Dashwood felt sad for[2] her.

A few days later, a carriage rode up to the front door. Elinor thought it was Colonel Brandon. But it was Edward.

"I must remain calm," she said to herself.

1. **indeed** [ɪn`diːd] (adv.) 確實
2. **feel sad for** 為……感到難過
3. **mumble** [`mʌmbəl] (v.) 含糊地說
4. **awful** [`ɔːfəl] (a.) 可怕的

He entered looking pale and nervous. Mrs. Dashwood greeted him kindly and congratulated him. He blushed and mumbled[3].

An awful[4] silence came over[5] the room. Mrs. Dashwood ended it by telling him she hoped Mrs. Ferrars was well.

"Is Mrs. Ferrars in Delaford?" Elinor bravely[6] asked.

"Delaford!" he said with surprise. "My mother is in London."

"I meant your new wife," Elinor said.

Edward hesitated[7]. "Perhaps you mean. . . my brother's new wife."

"Your brother's new wife?" Marianne and her mother repeated together with astonishment[8]. Elinor couldn't speak.

"Yes," Edward said, "My brother is now married to Miss Lucy Steele."

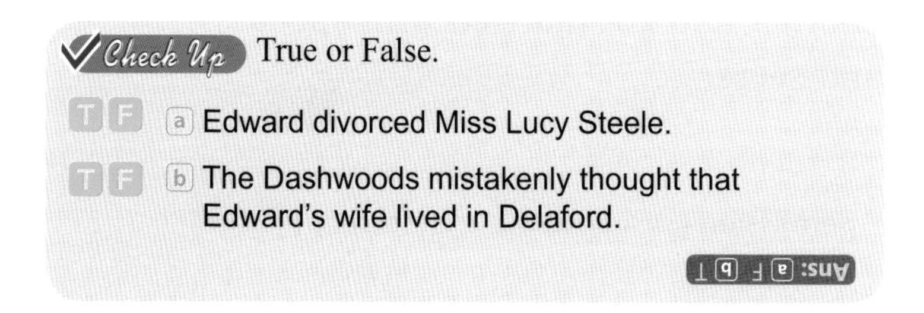

5. **come over** 突然影響；抓住
6. **bravely** [ˋbreɪvli] (adv.) 勇敢地
7. **hesitate** [ˋhezɪteɪt] (v.) 猶豫
8. **astonishment** [əˋstɑːnɪʃmənt] (n.) 驚愕

47

Elinor ran out of the room and burst into tears of happiness. Edward watched her run away and followed her.

The ladies were astonished. When they all sat down for tea, Edward asked for Mrs. Dashwood's permission[1] to marry Elinor. She said yes. He was the happiest man alive[2].

"My foolish engagement would not have happened if my mother had let me choose my own profession. I imagined myself in love. When I met you Elinor, I realized how wrong it was."

Everyone was delighted. He explained that his brother had visited Lucy, trying to persuade her to break off the engagement with his brother. Lucy realized that Robert, rather than Edward, would inherit his mother's fortune. Since they were both of a similarly[3] selfish character, they became attracted to[4] one another and got married with speed and secrecy[5].

1. **permission** [pər`mɪʃən] (n.) 同意
2. **alive** [ə`laɪv] (a.) 活著的
3. **similarly** [`sɪmɪlərli] (adv.) 同樣地
4. **attracted to** 吸引的
5. **secrecy** [`siːkrəsi] (n.) 祕密性
6. **horrified** [`hɔːrɪfaɪd] (a.) 驚懼的
7. **eventually** [ɪ`ventʃuəli] (adv.) 最終地

Edward's mother was horrified[6], but eventually[7] accepted it. She wasn't happy about Edward's engagement to Elinor, either, but she gave them 10,000 pounds. The money would allow Edward and Elinor to marry very soon and move into the minister's cottage at Delaford. They were the happiest couple in the world.

Moving to Delaford did not separate Elinor from[1] her sister. By the time Marianne was nineteen, with feelings of warm friendship[2] and respect, she agreed to marry Colonel Brandon, a man she had once considered dull[3] and too old.

Colonel Brandon was as happy now as everybody else. In time, Marianne came to love him as much as she had loved Willoughby.

Mrs. Dashwood kept living at Barton Cottage. As soon as Margaret grew old enough for dancing and parties, she visited Sir John and Mrs. Jennings. Barton and Delaford were connected and filled with[4] strong family affection. Elinor and Marianne lived very happily with their husbands and were very close to each other. As the years passed, the sisters became ever closer.

How did Marianne's feelings toward Colonel Brandon change?

a From disgust to weary surrender
b From contempt to respect
c From warm and friendly to hatred

Ans: b

1. **separate *A* from *B***
使 A 離開 B
2. **friendship** [ˋfrɛndʃɪp] (n.)
友情
3. **dull** [dʌl] (a.) 無聊的
4. **filled with** 充滿

A True or False.

T F ❶ Colonel Brandon was once in love with his distant cousin.

T F ❷ Mrs. Ferrars was very happy when she heard that Edward was engaged to Lucy Steele.

T F ❸ Colonel Brandon offered Edward Ferrars a job as a minister.

T F ❹ The Palmers' home was two days away from Barton.

B Choose the correct usage.

❶ (a) Elinor looked upon him with great sympathy.
(b) She sympathy the long journey that lay ahead.

❷ (a) The old lady praised Lucy's warm heart attentively.
(b) Marianne listened attentively and accepted Willoughby's guilt.

C Choose the correct answer.

1. Why did Eliza disappear for eight months?
   - (a) She went on a trip around the world.
   - (b) She was pregnant with Willoughby's baby without being married.
   - (c) She was kidnapped by bad men.
2. Why did Elinor burst into tears of happiness?
   - (a) She learned that Robert, not Edward, had married Lucy.
   - (b) Colonel Brandon gave Edward a job.
   - (c) She found out that Willoughby still loved Marianne.

D Rearrange the following sentences in chronological order.

1. Marianne called out for her mother in the middle of the night.
2. The doctor said Marianne would recover in a few days.
3. Colonel Brandon drove all night to fetch Mrs. Dashwood.
4. Willoughby came to explain his bad behavior.
5. The doctor admitted that his medicines failed to cure Marianne's fever.

______ ⇨ ______ ⇨ ______ ⇨ ______ ⇨ ______

Appendix 1

Guide to Listening Comprehension

When listening to the story, use some of the techniques shown below. If you take time to study some phonetic characteristics of English, listening will be easier.

Get in the flow of English.

English creates a rhythm formed by combinations of strong and weak stress intonations. Each word has its particular stress that combines with other words to form the overall pattern of stress or rhythm in a particular sentence.

When you are speaking and listening to English, it is essential to get in the flow of the rhythm of English. It takes a lot of practice to get used to such a rhythm. So, you need to start by identifying the stressed syllable in a word.

Listen for the strongly stressed words and phrases.

In English, key words and phrases that are essential to the meaning of a sentence are stressed louder. Therefore, pay attention to the words stressed with a higher pitch. When listening to an English recording for the first time, what matters most is to listen for a general understanding of what you hear. Do not try to hear every single word. Most of the unstressed words are articles or auxiliary verbs, which don't play an important role in the general context. At this level, you can ignore them.

Pay attention to liaisons.

In reading English, words are written with a space between them. There isn't such an obvious guide when it comes to listening to English. In oral English, there are many cases when the sounds of words are linked with adjacent words.

For instance, let's think about the phrase "take off," which can be used in "take off your clothes." "Take off your clothes" doesn't sound like [teɪk ɔːf] with each of the words completely and clearly separated from the others. Instead, it sounds as if almost all the words in context are slurred together, [ˋteɪkɔːf], for a more natural sound.

Shadow the voice of the native speaker.

Finally, you need to mimic the voice of the native speaker. Once you are sure you know how to pronounce all the words in a sentence, try to repeat them like an echo. Listen to the book again, but this time you should try a fun exercise while listening to the English.

This exercise is called "shadowing." The word "shadow" means a dark shade that is formed on a surface. When used as a verb, the word refers to the action of following someone or something like a shadow. In this exercise, pretend you are a parrot and try to shadow the voice of the native speaker.

Try to mimic the reader's voice by speaking at the same speed, with the same strong and weak stresses on words, and pausing or stopping at the same points.

Experts have already proven this technique to be effective. If you practice this shadowing exercise, your English speaking and listening skills will improve by leaps and bounds. While shadowing the native speaker, don't forget to pay attention to the meaning of each phrase and sentence.

Listen to what you want to shadow many times. Start out by just trying to shadow a few words or a sentence.

Mimic the CD out loud. You can shadow everything the speaker says as if you are singing a round, or you also can speak simultaneously with the recorded voice of the native speaker.

As you practice more, try to shadow more. For instance, shadow a whole sentence or paragraph instead of just a few words.

Listening Guide

Chapter One page 14–15 49

The Dashwoods (❶) ( ) the Southern English town of Sussex for many generations. They owned a large country house named Norland Park. The head of the family was old Mr. Dashwood, an elderly unmarried (❷). During the last years of Mr. Dashwood's life he invited his nephew, Henry Dashwood, and his family to move into Norland Park.

Henry Dashwood had one son, John, by his (❸) ( ) and three daughters by his present wife. John was a young man who had received a large inheritance from his mother. The Norland fortune was not as important to John as it was to his sisters, who had little money of their own.

When old Mr. Dashwood died, Henry (❹) ( ) his uncle had not left the fortune to him, but rather for him to use during his lifetime. When Henry died, the inheritance (❺) pass to his son John and then to John's son. This was because old Mr. Dashwood had been especially fond of John's son. But out of kindness, the old man left Henry's daughters 1,000 pounds each.

一開始若能聽清楚發音，之後就沒有聽力的負擔。首先，請聽過摘錄的章節，之後再反覆聆聽括弧內單字的發音，並仔細閱讀各種發音的說明。

以下都是以英語的典型發音為基礎，所做的簡易說明，即使這裡未提到的發音，也可以配合 CD 反覆聆聽，如此一來聽力必能更上層樓。

❶ **lived in**：lived 的 -d 以子音結尾，後接上母音開頭的 in，故產生連音，唸成 [lɪvdɪn]。

❷ **gentleman**：重音落於字首，唸成 [`dʒentlmən]。

❸ **first wife**：first 與其他字同發音時，因 -st 為吐氣音，故只需輕聲帶過即可。

❹ **learned that**：learned 字尾最後發音為 [d]，與後接的 th- 連音唸成 [`lɜːrnðæt]。

❺ **would**：could、would 與 should 三字的 -ould 都是 [ʊd] 的發音。

Chapter One page 16–17 (50)

Henry wanted the fortune for his (❶) ( ) ( ). But if he invested his money carefully, he (❷) ( ) enough to provide for them. Unfortunately, Henry suddenly died, unable to complete his plan. At this time, all that was left for his wife and daughters was 10,000 pounds.

Shortly (❸) his death, Henry begged his son John to take care of his stepmother and sisters. John did not have strong feelings for them, but he promised he would make them comfortable. He was not a bad man, but he was selfish and cold-hearted. His wife Fanny was even more selfish and cold-hearted than him.

(❹) ( ) ( ) Henry was buried, Fanny came to Norland Park uninvited. She rudely informed Mrs. Dashwood and her daughters that Norland Park was now hers and that they were her guests.

The recently widowed Mrs. Dashwood was terribly offended. She would have left the estate (❺) if her eldest daughter had not begged her to reconsider.

Elinor was the eldest daughter. She possessed (❻) ( ) and common sense. She was only nineteen, but she frequently advised her mother on important matters.

1. **wife and daughters**：wife 的 -fe 與 and 的 -a 開頭為連音；and 的 -d 又和 daughters 的 -d是相同子音 [d]，故可省略前個子音，全部一起唸為 [waɪfən`dɔːtərs]。

2. **would have**：would 的 -ld 在發音時僅需輕聲帶過，故兩字連在一起念成 [wʊhæv]。

3. **before**：before 的 be 發音為 [bɪ] 或 [bə]，不做強調作用時唸成 [bə`fɔːr]。

4. **As soon as**：as 的 -s 與後面 soon 的 s- 可連音；soon 的 -n 與後面 as 的 a- 也可連音，故全句發為 [əsuːnəz]。

5. **immediately**：immediately 和前個字 estate 為母音連音，故省略前個母音，唸成[ə`steɪtɪ`miːdiətli]。

6. **great intelligence**：great 為子音結尾，與後方 in- 母音相連，發成 [greɪtɪn`telɪdʒəns]。

Appendix 3

Listening Comprehension

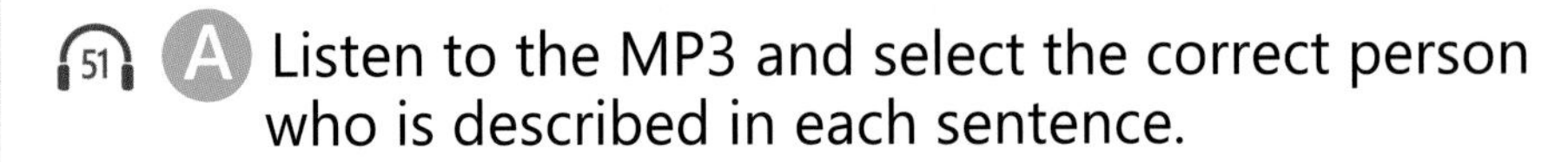

A Listen to the MP3 and select the correct person who is described in each sentence.

ⓐ Elinor ⓑ Marianne ⓒ Edward Ferrars ⓓ Willoughby

1. ______________________________ __________
2. ______________________________ __________
3. ______________________________ __________
4. ______________________________ __________

B Listen to the MP3 and fill in the blanks.

1. John received a large __________ from his mother.
2. Mrs. Dashwood __________ her __________ for his helping Marianne.
3. They found the Steele sisters __________ and __________.
4. This meeting __________ her __________ for him.

53 C Listen to the MP3 and choose the correct answer.

1 ________________________________?

(a) Because all of his friends married rich women.
(b) Because his income was small and his debts were great.
(c) Because he wanted to marry a woman with a big house so his horses could have their own bedroom.

2 ________________________________?

(a) He hunted him down and killed him.
(b) He told the police to arrest Willoughby.
(c) He challenged him to a duel for his dishonor.

54 D Listen to the MP3 and decide true or false.

T F 1 ________________________________

T F 2 ________________________________

T F 3 ________________________________

T F 4 ________________________________

T F 5 ________________________________

Translation

作者簡介 p. 4

珍・奧斯汀（Jane Austen，1775–1817）

珍・奧斯汀 1775 年 12 月 16 日生於英國漢普郡史蒂文頓堂區。她的父親喬治・奧斯汀是牧師，與其母親卡珊德拉・麗共有八個小孩，其中有兩個女孩，她排行第七，是第二個女兒。珍・奧斯汀與她的兄弟姊妹，以及寄宿家中、父親的家教學生們，一同度過快樂的童年。由於父親有間大圖書館，珍・奧斯汀還是小女孩時便常常受鼓勵，進行閱讀與寫作。

她的著作《理性與感性》（*Sense and Sensibility*, 1811）、《傲慢與偏見》（*Pride and Prejudice*, 1813）、《曼斯菲爾德莊園》（*Mansfield Park*, 1814）與《艾瑪》（*Emma*, 1815）自首次出版以來就頻繁再刷。

她的小說深刻描述當時英國中產階級百姓的愛與婚姻，因此十分受到推崇。不幸的是，珍・奧斯汀於 1817 年去世，享年 42 歲。她的遺作《諾桑覺寺》（*Northanger Abbey*）和《勸導》（*Persuasion*）於 1817 年末出版。

故事簡介

p. 5

《理性與感性》雖非珍·奧斯汀第一本小說，卻是第一本以筆名「一位女士」（A Lady）出版的作品，原書名為《依莉諾與瑪麗安》（*Elinor and Marianne*）。小說背景為 18 世紀的英國，描述戴西伍姊妹和婚姻相關的愛情與衝突。依莉諾代表了書名中的「理性」，而瑪麗安則代表「感性」。小說表現兩位姊妹如何經歷一些困難而臻至成熟。

戴西伍一家住在英國的北國莊園。戴西伍太太是先生的第二任妻子，先生死後，她與三個女兒（依莉諾、瑪麗安與瑪格麗）面對困苦的生活。戴西伍先生大多的遺產都給了第一段婚姻生的兒子：約翰·戴西伍。約翰答應父親會好好照顧繼母與妹妹，但自私的妻子芬妮不許約翰把應得的部分遺產給她們。戴西伍太太和女兒們在自己家中，卻如不被歡迎的賓客，幸好一位遠房親戚願意出租小屋給她們。

瑪麗安被布蘭登上校和威洛比求婚，但瑪麗安對三十好幾、個性安靜的上校沒興趣，喜歡面貌英俊的威洛比。依莉諾倒是早就受芬妮的哥哥愛德華吸引。愛德華是個沈靜紳士的男人，依莉諾欽佩他的智識與品味。在經歷過浪漫與心碎，兩位姊妹找到了各自的真愛與幸福。

角色簡介 p. 12–13

Elinor 依莉諾

我是三姊妹中的大姊，依莉諾。母親是戴西伍夫人，父親為亨利．戴西伍，他在壯年時便驟然過世，因此我要振作，好照顧母親與妹妹們，不能為情緒控制，不然會徒增家中困擾。

Marianne 瑪麗安

喔……何時能遇見真愛呢？我尋覓一位年輕英俊的紳士讓我一見傾心，富不富有都沒關係。我真搞不懂大姊依莉諾，明明深愛著愛德華．斐洛，卻隱藏心意。喔，如果是我，一定會表現出來！

Edward Ferrars 愛德華．斐洛

我不是個胸懷大志的男人，我的家人要我在社會上出人頭地，但我卻嚮往簡單、隱私的生活。即使放棄心愛的女子，還是要追求平靜生活。

Willoughby 威洛比

帥氣、迷人又年輕的我，也許有些花心，卻沒什麼錢，所以一定要娶個有錢、能養我的女人。

Colonel Brandon 布蘭登上校

我不是個膽小、害羞的人，只是沉默了點。我想我可能愛上瑪麗安了吧，但她最近愛上了威洛比，他是個渾蛋，但我目前不會戳破他，因為我不希望她被任何人傷害。

[第一章] 戴西伍一家

p. 14–15 戴西伍一家定居於英格蘭南部的薩克西斯鎮已經好幾代了，擁有一棟叫「北國莊園」的鄉間小屋。家中的主人是老戴西伍先生，一位年邁未婚的紳士。在老戴西伍先生在世的最後幾年，他邀請姪兒亨利・戴西伍一家人住進北國莊園。

亨利・戴西伍有個前妻生的兒子約翰，與現任妻子所生的三個女兒。年輕的約翰從母親身上繼承大筆財產，所以北國莊園的資產對他而言，沒有對比他拮据的姊妹們來得重要。

當老戴西伍先生去世，亨利發現叔叔並沒給他一筆財富，而是只夠他在生前用完而已。亨利死去後，資產會由約翰繼承，再傳給約翰的兒子，因為老戴西伍先生與約翰的兒子特別投緣。雖然如此，出於好意，他還是留給亨利每個女兒各一千英鎊。

p. 16–17 亨利想替妻子與女兒們多掙些錢。要是他有善加投資，就足夠撫養她們。不幸的是，他驟然離世，計畫是無法達成了。此時的他能留給妻子和女兒的，只剩下一萬英鎊。

還未離世前，亨利懇求約翰好好照顧繼母與妹妹們，雖然約翰對她們感情不深，還是保證讓她們衣食無缺。約翰不算壞，但個性自私又冷酷，而他的妻子芬妮，比他要來得更加自私冷酷。

亨利下葬後，芬妮不請自來到了北國莊園，無禮地向戴西伍夫人宣示房屋主權，更說戴西伍夫人與女兒不過是她的房客。

剛失去丈夫的戴西伍夫人感覺被嚴重冒犯了，要不是長女請求她再三考慮，她一定馬上離開這裡。

長女依莉諾聰穎有見識，雖然年僅十九歲，卻已能夠向母親建議許多重要事情。

p. 18–19 依莉諾擁有母親與妹妹瑪麗安所欠缺的特質——自制力。

瑪麗安與依莉諾一樣地大方、聰穎與敏感，但她情緒易起伏，感情外放，這點倒是和母親很相似。

年紀最小的瑪格麗，是個甜甜的十三歲女生，情緒和瑪麗安一樣豐沛，卻少了那份聰明。

有天，約翰．戴西伍提醒妻子，要履行在父親生前做的承諾。他說他想要給每位妹妹一人一千英鎊，但芬妮卻反對這贈予。

她說：「你這樣會讓我們將來的孩子少了三千英鎊的遺產。你跟她們只有一半血緣，她們根本不算是你的妹妹。」

「她們要搬新家了，我該幫點忙。不然每個人五百英磅好了。」約翰回答。

「不用那麼多，」芬妮討價還價說：「你太大方了啦，我想她們靠你父親留下的一萬英鎊，日子就很好過了。」

「也是，還是每年給我繼母一百英鎊就好？」約翰回答。

p. 20–21 「好啊。但我不認為你父親是叫你給她們錢，」芬妮答：「他是要你替她們找個舒服的小窩，幫忙搬遷，偶爾送上一簍鮮魚或是肉。馬車跟馬匹也不用，一兩個傭人就好，再多就很愚蠢了。」

「我想妳是對的！現在我懂父親的意思了。」約翰說。

他決定依妻子所建議的提供她們幫助。

在這期間，寡婦戴西伍夫人只想盡快離開北國莊園。她對媳婦非常反感，留在這裡的唯一理由，是因為長女依莉諾與芬妮的哥哥——愛德華．斐洛，有很深的感情 。

愛德華的父親過世後，留下大筆遺產，但他不確定誰會得到，這由他的母親決定。但戴西伍夫人不在意他的財富，她的女兒與愛德華似乎深深相愛。

p. 22–23 愛德華．斐洛不特別英俊或是特別紳士，就是個善良害羞的人。母親與妹妹希望他能在社會上出人頭地，但他沒那種野心。平靜安穩的生活，才是他的唯一嚮往。他的弟弟羅伯特還比較有潛力。

「愛德華與依莉諾幾個月後可能會結婚。」戴西伍夫人告訴瑪麗安說：「妳不認同愛德華嗎？」

「他眼中沒有熱情，看起來也不懂閱讀和音樂。唉……如何才能遇見我真愛的人呢？」瑪麗安擔心說道。

「妳才十七歲！」戴西伍夫人笑言：「現在就失去信心還太早了呢。」

依莉諾很欣賞愛德華，但還不確定是否要嫁給他。他常常看起來心事重重。她擔心他只將她當成朋友而已。

瑪麗安與母親倒是沒這層顧慮，她們相信愛情能戰勝一切。聽到姊姊形容她對愛德華的感覺是尊重而非愛情時，瑪麗安覺得真是糟糕。「喜歡他？尊敬他？喔，冷冷的依莉諾！為什麼要羞於表達感情呢？」

p. 24–25 注意到愛德華與依莉諾之間的情感，芬妮坐立不安。她告訴她的婆婆戴西伍夫人說：「我與我母親都盼望愛德華能娶得很好，依莉諾要是想騙愛德華娶她，可是會很危險的喔！」

芬妮的話讓戴西伍夫人憤怒極了，決定要帶著女兒們馬上離開北國莊園。

就在當天，戴西伍夫人收到遠親約翰·彌德頓先生的來信，他願意提供他在德文島郡地產附近的小屋供她們居住。這封信充滿歡迎之意，戴西伍夫人立刻回信，欣然接受。

戴西伍夫人開心地告訴約翰和芬妮，她們要離開北國莊園，搬到德文島郡。

當時也在屋中的愛德華·斐洛忽然轉過身說：「德文島郡！離這裡很遠呢。」

「是啊，」她回答：「我們會在離愛塞特城四哩外的巴頓住下。雖然只是間小房子，還是希望到時你會來拜訪我們。」

戴西伍夫人對愛德華的邀請是由衷親切的，她並不想阻擋他與依莉諾的感情。

p. 26–27 巴頓小屋已裝修過，能讓她們立即入住。依莉諾建議母親將馬車與馬匹賣掉，留下三名傭人即可。

亨利臨終前曾告訴妻子，約翰承諾會照顧她和女兒的。但當她們離開時，一切化為泡影。實際上，反而是約翰在抱怨自己錢不夠用。

離開深愛的北國莊園時，三姊妹都哭了，「別了，親愛的北國莊園，」瑪麗安最後一晚在莊園中獨自漫步時說：「我會一輩子想念你的！」

前往德文島郡途中，她們難抑悲傷，無法享受旅程；但到達巴頓谷後，她們情緒好轉，開始注意將要居住地點的鄉間風光。巴頓谷有茂密的樹林、清澈溪流與遼闊原野。

巴頓小屋的屋況甚佳，四房兩廳，還有兩間僕人房，雖然比北國莊園狹小、樸素得多，女孩們還是苦中作樂。

p. 28–29 隔天，房東約翰・彌德頓先生登門拜訪。他是個英俊又開朗的人。他歡迎她們，並提供家裡和花園的所有物品。他的房子名為「巴頓莊園」。他努力讓她們盡量過得舒適，並說希望她們能盡快到他家中拜訪。

隔天，她們來到約半哩路程遠的巴頓莊園用晚膳，那可真是個豪華的房子，彌德頓一家必定住得很舒服。約翰先生是愛好射擊的運動家，彌德頓夫人則是個溺愛孩子的母親。

約翰先生很好客，總是喜歡呼朋引伴到家中，越熱鬧越好，巴頓莊園的夏日宴會與冬季舞會更是相當出名。

夜晚，戴西伍一家到達莊園。約翰先生致歉，因為現場沒有英俊的年輕男士，而只有他的朋友，也就是暫住在他家的布蘭登上校，與約翰的岳母潔寧絲夫人。

p. 30–31 潔寧絲夫人是位多話愛笑的豐腴老夫人；布蘭登上校則嚴肅寡言，面貌英俊。依莉諾與瑪麗安注意到他是個年過三十五歲的老單身漢。

晚餐後，瑪麗安彈奏鋼琴與唱歌，約翰先生高調地表現出對音樂的興趣，布蘭登上校在一旁安靜專注地聆聽。

潔寧絲夫人是個不愁吃穿的寡婦，見到自己兩個女兒嫁得好，就恨不得把全世界的其他女孩都嫁出去。她花許多精神在撮合年輕男女，籌備婚禮。

她向彌德頓一家和戴西伍一家說，布蘭登上校迷戀著瑪麗安，她認為兩人郎「財」女貌，是美事一樁。

「潔寧絲夫人這樣說多傷人啊，」瑪麗安說：「布蘭登上校老得可以做我爸了！」

「但一個小我五歲的人，有你說的這麼老嗎？」戴西伍夫人回答。

「妳沒聽到他抱怨自己的背不好嗎？」瑪麗安說。

p. 32–33 「孩子啊，」戴西伍夫人笑言：「我活到四十歲這把歲數，對妳而言很神奇吧。三十五歲無礙結婚。打個比方，一個二十七歲的女人，自然地就會考慮嫁給像布蘭登上校這樣年紀的人。」

「要是一個二十七歲的女人家境貧寒，倒是可以考慮當他的護士，來個實惠的婚姻。」

「他不過是抱怨天氣濕冷，肩膀痠疼，這樣就說他需要看護，未免太刻薄囉。」依莉諾說。

但瑪麗安還是沒有改變對布蘭登上校的看法。依莉諾離開房間後，瑪莉安說：「媽，我擔心愛德華．斐洛是不是病了。來這裡都兩星期了，他卻還沒來看依莉諾。」

「別急，孩子。」戴西伍夫人回答：「我沒想過他會這麼快來，依莉諾也是。」

「真是太奇怪了，」瑪麗安驚呼：「他們上次道別時，竟然那麼冷漠平靜！依莉諾總是那麼有自制力，不會難過、不安或悲傷，好令人難懂。」

[第二章] 英俊的陌生人

p. 36–37 戴西伍姊妹總算開始習慣巴頓小屋的生活。這是自從父親去世以後，她們第一次又喜歡上散步和練習音樂。沒有多少人來拜訪她們，附近走路能抵達的房舍也不多。附近唯一一幢房屋，是一哩外的艾倫漢大宅。聽說屋主史密斯夫人是一位身體欠安的年長女士，所以也沒有辦法接待訪客。

某日，瑪麗安與瑪格麗不顧依莉諾警告將有豪雨，就跑到屋後的山丘上。她們在山頂上注視著蔚藍天空和白色雲朵，感覺非常愉快。風拂過髮絲，彼此都笑了，「這是世界上最棒的地方！」瑪麗安大喊。

但沒幾分鐘後，烏雲密佈，雨水傾瀉而下。兩人急忙下山，瑪格麗跑在前頭，沒看見瑪麗安失足滑倒。

此時，一位外出打獵的紳士看見這意外，並上前幫忙。瑪麗安扭傷膝蓋，無法站立，紳士便送她回巴頓小屋，將她置於沙發上。

p. 38–39 依莉諾和母親看到陌生人抱著瑪麗安進屋時，都嚇到了。兩人注意到他英俊的外表，他則是為自己無禮的闖入感到抱歉。戴西伍夫人隨後感謝他幫助了瑪麗安。

她詢問對方姓名，知道他叫威洛比，現居於艾倫漢大宅。威洛比說他明天會再來探視瑪麗安，戴西伍夫人則表示隨時歡迎威洛比的來訪。然後威洛比便離去，消失在滂沱大雨中。

依莉諾與母親相當喜歡這年輕人，但因為腳傷，瑪麗安根本沒見到他。她熱切地想著她的英雄，幾乎忘記腳踝的傷。

約翰先生來訪時，被問到是否知道艾倫漢大宅的威洛比。

「威洛比！當然知道囉！」他大聲說：「他每年都來看我們。星期四找他來用晚餐好了。」

「他人怎樣？」戴西伍夫人問。

「人很好，射擊技術精湛，還是全英國最好的騎士。」

她們問了更多個人資料，約翰先生便告訴她們，威洛比在德文島郡沒有置產，來訪都是住在親戚史密斯女士的艾倫漢大宅中，還說他可能會繼承那老夫人的財富。

p. 40–41 瑪麗安的救命恩人隔天早晨來訪。威洛比和戴西伍一家越漸熟稔。瑪麗安眼中的愛火，像是要把他吞噬般。他們分享興趣、天南地北聊著，在她離開之前，兩人暢談得像是認識許久的老友一般。

之後，威洛比每天都到巴頓小屋拜訪。一開始他還會假裝關心瑪麗安的傷勢，後來馬上就不裝了，公開地享受她的陪伴。兩個人一起閱讀、唱歌和聊天。

瑪麗安認為，威洛比擁有愛德華·斐洛所欠缺的所有感性與品味。很快地，她認定了他就是自己的完美伴侶，且威洛比似乎也這麼想。戴西伍夫人暗自恭喜自己將要有個好女婿了。

與此同時，依莉諾開始同情起布蘭登上校。上校輸給了一位二十五歲的青年，沒能贏得瑪麗安的愛。瑪麗安和威洛比以嘲笑布蘭登上校為樂，這也讓依莉諾感到沮喪。

依莉諾不快樂，她無法停止思念她在舊家薩西克斯郡的朋友，而她唯一能傾訴的人，僅有喜歡談論瑪麗安的布蘭登上校。

p. 42–43 「我看妳妹妹無心展開第二段情吧。」布蘭登上校說。

「她啊，滿腦袋羅曼蒂克思想，相信一生只有一次真愛。希望她會理智點。」

「那事真有可能會發生的，」布蘭登繼續說：「我知道曾經有個年輕女孩……」

他突然停住，覺得自己太過多嘴了。依莉諾猜想那一定是段挫折的愛情，就更同情他了。

隔天，瑪格麗對依莉諾說：「有個大祕密！我昨晚撞見威洛比向瑪麗安要一綹頭髮。瑪麗安剪下一撮給他，他親吻頭髮後就放進口袋中。」

依莉諾猜他們是私定終身了，也驚訝他們竟沒向任何人透露。

隔天，約翰先生為大家計劃了趟旅行，要到「輝偉爾公館」去度假。公館是布蘭登上校姊夫的房子。他們一大夥人打包午餐餐點，準備出發。

p. 44–45 然而，早餐時，布蘭登上校接到一封信。他看了信後，向大家表示他有急事。

旅程被取消了。雖然大夥兒勸他先把事情擱著，但他不想這樣做。

布蘭登離開後，大家決定乘車瀏覽鄉間風光。瑪麗安則是坐上了威洛比的馬車，一整天不見兩人影子。

隔天一早，戴西伍夫人帶著兩個女兒拜訪彌德頓夫人，而瑪麗安因威洛比即將來訪而留在家中。

戴西伍夫人帶著女兒們回到家時，看見威洛比的馬車停在小屋外頭，她們並不意外。

但進到房中後，卻看到瑪麗安不能抑止地啜泣，之後便衝出客廳往樓上跑去。

「她不舒服嗎？」戴西伍夫人問威洛比。

「不是，」他試著愉快地回答：「但我有個壞消息。我親戚史密斯夫人要我到倫敦去出差，沒法子再來這兒了。我很窮，她是我的經濟來源，所以我得照她所說的辦。我是來道別的。」

p. 46–47 「那麼，希望你不要離開太久。」戴西伍夫人說。

「今年恐怕是回不來了。」他泛紅著臉回答。

戴西伍夫人驚訝地望著依莉諾，而她也很震驚的樣子。威洛比告別，急忙乘著馬車離去。依莉諾則擔心妹妹情緒化的個性 ，會讓她深陷痛苦。

那天稍晚，戴西伍夫人告訴依莉諾，或許史密斯夫人將威洛比送走的理由，是因為她不贊同他與瑪麗安的婚約。

「他一定會盡快回巴頓的。」

「那他們為什麼要隱瞞婚約？」依莉諾問。

「親愛的，」母親責難說：「妳怪他們隱瞞感情是很奇怪的！之前妳還不喜歡他們太直接表達情感呢！難道妳認為他對瑪麗安的意圖是壞的，而不是好的？」

「我不希望是壞的啊，」依莉諾大聲說：「但願他今天異常的舉止有個解釋。」

一直到晚餐時，大家才看見瑪麗安。餐桌上，她難過得無法進食，也無法抬頭看任何人。只要有人提到威洛比，她就會傷心地嚎啕大哭。

p. 48–49 接下來的幾天，瑪麗安的情況越來越糟。一週後，姊妹們勸她外出散心。散步時，她們看見有個男人朝她們駕車而來。

「是威洛比！我知道是他！」瑪麗安大喊，向馬車跑去。

來的不是威洛比，而是愛德華‧斐洛。不過他也是世上除了威洛以外，瑪麗安唯一想見的人了。她停下腳步，忍住快掉下的淚水，向他微笑。依莉諾與愛德華互相問候時，瑪麗安見識到他倆客套疏遠的行為。

他們回到小屋。戴西伍夫人溫柔地問候愛德華：「愛德華，這些日子來，你母親對你有什麼規畫嗎？依然堅持要你從政嗎？」

「不，她明白我做不到。我們無法在職業選擇上達成共識，我一直想替教會工作，但他們認為那太沒出息。」愛德華答。

「我知道你事業心不強，愛德華。」戴西伍夫人說。

「是的。我只想像其他人一樣，好好享受自己喜愛的生活。成名並不會讓我開心。」

「你說的對極了！」瑪麗安驚呼：「財富與名聲，和幸福有什麼關聯呢？」

依莉諾說：「或許名聲與幸福沒什麼關係，但金錢關係可大了。」

p. 50–51 「依莉諾！」瑪麗安大吼：「什麼都無法給予時，才只能由金錢得到快樂；除了滿足基本需求外，錢根本就沒有用處。」

「那你需要多少錢滿足基本需求？」依莉諾問。

「一年兩千鎊就夠，不用再多了。」瑪麗安說。

依莉諾笑了，她說：「兩千鎊！一年有一千鎊，我就要偷笑了。」

「一個家庭的開銷，一年無法少於兩千鎊，」瑪麗安說：「要有足夠的僕人、一輛馬車與幾匹馬，就是需要這麼多錢。」

依莉諾聽著妹妹形容往後與威洛比的生活，笑了出來。

愛德華來訪期間，依莉諾依然是一貫的有禮與關懷。但她察覺到，他對她很冷淡，一副不甚開心的樣子，她開始懷疑他是否還愛她。她能瞧見他眼中的疑慮。

隔天用午茶時，依莉諾注意到愛德華手上戴了只戒指。

「愛德華，我從沒看過這個耶！戒指上的頭髮，是你妹妹的嗎？」

他臉紅，很快瞄了依莉諾一眼回答說：「是啊，是芬妮的頭髮，看起來比平常還要柔亮。」

依莉諾確定他一定趁她不知道時，拿了些她一些頭髮。

p. 52–53

理智 vs. 情感

書名中的「理性」與「感性」這對比的主題，不只存在於此書中，也存在於小說寫成的那個年代。依莉諾與瑪麗安這兩位主角，分別代表這兩種對比。每位女性對自己愛人的方式不盡相同，一種是像依莉諾般，隱藏內心情感，甚少對所愛的愛德華·斐洛表達關心之情；另一種如瑪麗安，熱切無懼地表現出對威洛比的迷戀。

這兩種截然不同的特點，反映出「理性」和「感性」的不同處。「理性」指的當然是「人之常情」，就是「以比較實際理智的方法來處裡事情」；「感性」最概括地說，就是「以情感為主宰」。

奧斯汀描述這兩個相反特質的行為時，可能是受當時社會變遷的影響。古典主義作為啟蒙運動中的其中一個文化潮流，那時即將來到尾聲，依莉諾的思想與行為就有古典主義的風格。而浪漫主義的崛起，則是呼應在瑪麗安的行事風格上。但奧斯汀不只是對比這兩種個性。依莉諾也有熱情的一面，且瑪麗安在故事結局還理智了起來。奧斯汀可能是想讓讀者思考理性與感性各自的好壞，並承認我們都是理性、感性兼具的人。

[第三章] 祕密

p. 54-55 約翰先生在巴頓莊園的客人增加了。他最近認識了遠房親戚史帝爾家的兩位年輕姊妹，便邀請她們至園中參觀，而她們也立即欣然答應。

戴西伍家姊妹倆在巴頓莊園見到約翰先生的新客人，覺得史帝爾家姊妹文雅美麗。姊姊安妮面貌平平，妹妹露西則是個二十三歲的美人。

「戴西伍小姐，」史帝爾家的姊姊問：「您喜歡德文島郡嗎？離開美麗的北國莊園一定很難過吧。」

依莉諾對她們知道自己家的事，感到訝異。她回答：「是啊，那裡是個好地方。」

「那妳一定認識很多英俊的單身漢！」安妮說。

「我的天呀，安妮，你就滿腦子的男人！」露西大聲斥責。

對話結束後，依莉諾鬆了口氣。她覺得那位姊姊盡說些庸俗瑣事；妹妹心機深不可測。這對姊妹個性截然不同。不久後她們熟稔起來，每天聚在一起一兩個小時。

p. 56–57 約翰先生向史帝爾一家人全盤托出戴西伍家的生活。有一天，安妮．史帝爾向依莉諾道賀，說恭喜瑪麗安和一位年輕的英俊男士訂婚了，還說約翰先生說過，依莉諾可能愛慕著愛德華。

「他姓斐洛，」約翰先生私語：「這可是個大祕密！」

安妮．史帝爾複述：「是你大嫂的哥哥，斐洛先生嗎？我們和他很熟呢。」

「妳怎麼這樣說話，安妮？」總是糾正姊姊的露西大喊：「我們和斐洛先生不過在叔叔家中見過一兩次而已。」

依莉諾感到震驚，想追問她們的叔叔是誰，又是怎麼知道愛德華的，但她忍住了。

接下來幾天，露西不停找依莉諾說話。她是個幽默機智的夥伴，但依莉諾同情她缺乏教育，不喜歡她隱藏於言語行為之間的虛偽、不正直與自私自利。

她們同肩並行時，露西問：「這麼問可能很奇怪，不過妳認識妳嫂子的母親——斐洛夫人嗎？」

p. 58–59 這問題對依莉諾而言，真是有些奇怪。「我沒見過她。」她冷漠地回答。

「所以妳不知道她是怎麼樣的人囉？」露西問。

「我不知道，」依莉諾淡淡地回應著，掩藏住她對愛德華母親的真正想法：「我完全不了解她。」

露西看著依莉諾說：「要是能告訴妳我現在處境多困難就好了！」

「我也希望能幫妳，但我真的跟斐洛夫人不熟。」

「斐洛夫人還不知道我，」露西橫瞥依莉諾一眼，害羞地說：「但不久後我們就會成為姻親了。」

「妳是說妳要跟羅伯特．斐洛先生結婚嗎？天啊！」依莉諾驚呼。

她可不想與露西成為妯娌。

「不，」露西答：「不是羅伯特，我這輩子還沒見過他呢。我指的是他的哥哥，愛德華。」

依莉諾驚訝地無法言語。

「很訝異吧，」露西說：「因為他未曾向你們提到我們的關係，不過愛德華不會氣我跟妳說這個祕密的。他一向視妳們為姊妹，對妳們很信任。」

依莉諾強迫自己保持冷靜，她說：「我能請問你們訂婚多久了嗎？」

「我們訂婚到現在四年了。」露西回答。

依莉諾不敢相信。

p. 60–61 「我是在他於德文島郡讀法律時認識他的」露西說：「我不想未經他母親的允許就私訂終身，但那時年輕的我深愛著他。喔……親愛的愛德華。妳看，我隨身帶著他的照片。」

她從口袋裡拿出愛德華的小張畫像給依莉諾瞧，依莉諾的心一沉。

「妳絕對無法想像我的苦楚，」露西接著說：「我們不常見面。」

露西用手掩住雙眼，依莉諾毫無反應。

「有時候真想結束，」露西繼續說：「可我沒法傷害他，妳說呢？」

「妳自己決定吧。」依莉諾回答。

「他連我的照片都沒有，」露西繼續說：「但我寄給他一枚有我髮絲纏繞在上的戒指。最近他拜訪妳時，有見他戴著嗎？」

「有。」依莉諾回答。平靜的聲音，隱藏著她心中極度的不悅，其實她是很震撼、困惑與悲傷的。

談話結束後，依莉諾覺得愛德華依然愛她，不會存心欺騙她。他不過是被一個美麗虛偽、庸俗自私的女子所設計，而對方在乎的是他未來優渥的收入。

p. 62–63 依莉諾很小心地隱藏起低落的情緒。她知道，要是家人知道這件關於愛德華的壞消息，她們的悲傷也只會徒增她的難過。

她幾次平靜地告訴露西事情的原委。依莉諾發現，露西一心想套牢愛德華，因為她忌妒愛德華是如此地看重依莉諾。她告訴依莉諾這個祕密，除了要她遠離愛德華，難道還會有別的目的嗎？

最讓依莉諾痛心的就是，她知道愛德華根本不愛未來的妻子，也無法擁有幸福的婚姻。

打算回倫敦的潔寧絲夫人，出乎意料地邀請依莉諾與瑪麗安前去。

「妳們一定要來，」她對戴西伍姊妹說：「我最會替單身女郎找丈夫了。要是沒至少將妳們其中一個嫁出去，可不是我的問題喔！」

依莉諾擔心可能會在倫敦碰見愛德華和露西．史帝爾，本想回絕這邀請，但瑪麗安興奮雀躍，因為她有機會在倫敦看見威洛比。戴西伍夫人堅持她們前來。

p. 64–65 抵達潔寧絲夫人位於倫敦的豪華宅第房內後，她倆拿出紙筆開始寫信。

「我會寫信回家給母親，」依莉諾對瑪麗安說：「妳或許可以拖個幾天再寫。」

「我不是寫給媽媽。」瑪麗安答。

依莉諾才發現她在寫信給威洛比。接下來的夜晚，瑪麗安處於緊張狀態，食不下嚥，焦慮地聽著每輛駛過的馬車聲。晚餐後，有人敲門，她跳起來大喊：「一定是威洛比！」

她衝向門口，整個人幾乎撞進布蘭登上校的懷中。她驚訝得無法自持，便離開了房間。依莉諾招呼著上校，看見如此深愛妹妹的人，得到的竟只有對方眼中苦澀的失望，依莉諾深感遺憾。

「瑪麗安不舒服嗎？」上校問。

依莉諾說了幾個像是疲倦頭痛之類的藉口。潔寧絲夫人愉快地走進房內，詢問上校去了哪些地方。

上校禮貌地回答，但沒講出什麼明白的答案。不久後，他離去，大家也就早早就寢。

p. 66–67 隔日，瑪麗安滿心期待地等候威洛比，整天心不在焉。 但女孩們購物結束回來時，仍然沒有他的消息。在潔寧絲夫人家中的一個禮拜後，她們終於在外出歸來時，看見了桌上有威洛比寄來的卡片。

瑪麗安驚呼:「我們不在時他來過了！」自那時起，其他人外出時，她都留在屋中。

次日捎來了封信，瑪麗安試著搶先拿走，但那信其實是給潔寧絲夫人的。

「妳在等誰的信嗎？」依莉諾問，她看出妹妹的失落。

「算吧。」她嘆息。

「親愛的，妳不相信我嗎？」依莉諾問。

「不信任所有人的妳，竟問我這問題？」瑪麗安回答。

「我沒有什麼好說的！」依莉諾咆哮著，她好想說出露西和愛德華婚約。

「我也沒有。」瑪麗安答：「妳不說，那我也不告訴妳我隱瞞什麼。」

隔天，彌德頓夫人倫敦家中舉辦了舞會。瑪麗安發現威洛比沒來，也失去對舞會的興趣。威洛比明明受邀卻缺席，讓她十分受傷。

p. 68–69 一天晚上，戴西伍姊妹倆隨著彌德頓夫人來到宴會。威洛比出現了，身旁還站著一位美麗年輕的女子。瑪麗安看到他開心極了，正要奔向他，卻被依莉諾阻止了。

「冷靜點，」依莉諾說，「把妳的情緒收好。」

但瑪麗安根本做不到，在座位上的她，滿臉寫著焦躁與不耐煩。

「為什麼他不看我？」瑪麗安大聲說。

威洛比總算看見她們，徐步走來。瑪麗安衝向前想握住他的手，他卻朝依莉諾走去，問她們母親身體可好。

瑪麗安羞紅了臉，喊道：「威洛比，你怎麼沒來看我？」

「有啊，可是妳不在。」他回答。

「你沒收到我的信嗎？」她焦慮地問：「一定是出了什麼可怕的差錯。求求你告訴我，發生什麼事了？」

威洛比面露慚愧神情，瞄了先前站在身邊的女子一眼。

「我有收到妳說妳在倫敦，謝謝妳告訴我。」

說完，他轉身加入別人的談話。

p. 70–71 瑪麗安臉色發白，站不住腳。依莉諾攙扶著她到座位上。威洛比之後很快便離開了宴會。回家路上，依莉諾知道威洛比與瑪麗安的感情結束了，她對威洛比草率了結關係感到很不滿。

當天夜裡，依莉諾聽著瑪麗安的低泣聲，無法成眠。隔天，瑪麗安收到一封信。潔寧絲夫人問是否是情書，還說道：「我這輩子沒見過這麼癡情的女孩，希望他不會辜負她才好。」

依莉諾走進房內時，見到瑪麗安正在痛哭流涕。她握住瑪麗安的手，一同放聲大哭，隨後讀了對方的來信。

親愛的女士：

若您不認同昨夜我的作法，我只盼能獲得您的諒解。我會永遠記得我們之間曾有過的美好。希望我沒有讓您產生愛情的錯覺。很久以前我就與人訂下婚約，我們不久後就要結婚。我於信中歸還您曾好意贈與的髮絲。

友人約翰・威洛比敬上

p. 72–73 依莉諾對這無情、制式語氣的信感到噁心。這實在太傷人又殘忍了。那刻，她對於瑪麗安不用嫁給這種爛男人而慶幸。

「喔，依莉諾，抱歉讓妳難過了。」瑪麗安說。

「但妳想想，要是妳訂婚後才發現他醜陋的真面目，不知道妳會有多慘。」依莉諾回應。

「訂婚！」瑪麗安驚呼：「我們從未訂婚。他不曾給我任何承諾。」

「他說過愛妳嗎？」依莉諾問。

「從來沒有，但從他的眼神裡，我知道他愛我。」瑪麗安大聲說。

說完，又繼續哭泣。

之後，潔寧絲夫人過來關心過度傷心的瑪麗安，告訴她們威洛比的女友是葛瑞小姐，她一年收入高達五千英鎊。她還說，威洛比花太多錢在馬車和馬匹上，急切地需要用錢。她不齒他的作為，不過倒認為這是一勞永逸，因為現在瑪麗安能嫁給布蘭登上校了。

[第四章] 真相大白

p. 76–77 翌日，瑪麗安更加悲傷，決心要避開潔寧絲夫人。

「她根本不是同情我，」瑪麗安抱怨：「只是喜歡拿我的事，來跟朋友嚼舌根而已。」

早飯過後，潔寧絲夫人到房裡找兩姊妹，拿了封信給瑪麗安說：「親愛的，妳看了會開心喔。」

瑪麗安希望這是威洛比的道歉信，寫來解釋他的奇怪行為，但那是母親捎來的信，內容充滿對威洛比的信任之情。瑪麗安一想到母親知道真相後的失望，就又大哭起來。

一陣敲門聲傳來，原來是布蘭登上校。瑪麗安跑回房中，留下依莉諾招呼臉色不佳的上校。

「我是來和妳談談的。」布蘭登對依莉諾說：「我想告訴妳一些關於威洛比人品的事。」

「你所說的，證明了你對瑪麗安的感情。」依莉諾說。

「不知道妳是否記得，在巴頓莊園時，我向妳提過一位很像妳妹妹的女子。她有熱情積極的個性、慈悲心腸與極佳的感受力。她是我的遠親和青梅竹馬，就這樣我們相愛了。」布蘭登說。

p. 78–79 「她十七歲那年，被迫嫁給我哥。本來我們婚禮前要私奔，但我父親發現了，把我送進軍中。他們的婚姻很不幸，因為我哥與數不清的女子有染。兩年後他們離婚了。」

依莉諾關心憐惜地看著他。

他接下去說：「三年後，我在負債人待的監獄中找到她。她病得很重，時日不多，我照顧她直到她死在我懷裡。她留下一個女兒託我照顧，名叫伊莉莎。我送她去讀書，還請一位有名望的女士照顧她，到現在都十七歲了。可是去年，她忽然失蹤，整整八個月，我不停打探她的消息。」

「天啊！威洛比該不會……」依莉諾驚呼。

「妳記得在巴頓莊園那天嗎？我們大家本來打算要去透透氣，但我收到緊急的消息，需要離開。威洛比壓根不知道我是去幫助一位被他害慘的人，反正他也不在乎。他做了最下流的事，丟下他所誘拐的女孩，無依無靠，身無分文。」

p. 80–81 「這根本就是禽獸嘛！」依莉諾大聲說。

「現在妳知道他是哪種人了吧。見到妳妹妹為他那種人瘋狂，我真是難受極了，誰知道他居心何在？拿她的處境和我可憐的伊莉莎比一比，有天她會謝天謝地的。」

「你離開巴頓後，有見過威洛比嗎？」依莉諾問。

「有。當伊莉莎對我坦承，欺騙她感情的人正是他時，我看不起他的卑劣行徑，向他提出決鬥。我們兩人最後都沒受什麼傷。可憐的伊莉莎，懷了小孩，現居於鄉下。」

上校離開後，依莉諾詳述他們的對話給瑪麗安聽。她的反應不如預期，只是仔細聆聽，接受事實。知道威洛比不再善良，丟失良心，才更使她悲傷。

隔天，戴西伍夫人的回信到來。她建議女兒們不要提早從潔寧絲夫人那離開。太快歸來巴頓只會讓她們憶起與威洛比的快樂時光。

p. 82–83 約翰先生和潔寧絲夫人同聲譴責威洛比做出這種丟人的事，他們還認為依莉諾會是布蘭登上校未來的妻子。

收到威洛比信件的兩週後，依莉諾得知他已成婚。瑪麗安開始很平靜，但之後不禁嚎啕哭泣。

此刻，依莉諾不情願地與抵達倫敦的史帝爾姊妹碰面。露西裝得一副開心見到她的模樣，依莉諾得用盡力氣才能保持禮貌。

有更令人歡迎的客人來訪，那就是約翰．戴西伍。他也來到了潔寧絲夫人家中。

與布蘭登上校介紹認識後，他私下要求和依莉諾走走。約翰說：「依莉諾，恭喜妳快要嫁給好人家了，布蘭登上校最紳士了，我想一定對妳有意思。」

「他想娶的不是我。」她回答。

「妹妹，那妳就錯了，妳很容易就可以讓他愛上妳。如果芬妮的哥哥和我的妹妹同時成婚，那可真是有趣啊！」

「愛德華先生要結婚了嗎？」依莉諾平靜地問著。

p. 84–85 「還沒定呢，不過他將會娶摩頓小姐。她是摩頓勳爵唯一的掌上明珠，擁有三萬英鎊的身價。要是他們結婚，愛德華的母親每年會給他一千英磅。真希望我們的生活也能這麼優渥。」他說。

一週後，約翰和芬妮夫妻兩人辦了個晚宴，爾德頓一家、潔寧絲夫人、布蘭登上校、戴西伍姊妹與史帝爾姊妹都是座上賓。露西和依莉諾都曉得斐洛夫人會在場。

「喔天啊，戴西伍小姐，」在他們上階梯時，露西耳語道，「我馬上就要看見那位決定我幸福與否的人了——我未來的婆婆！」

斐洛夫人是個瘦弱、面貌刻薄的婦人，顯然她排斥依莉諾，對露西．史帝爾則表現出認同的樣子。

「要是她知道露西的祕密，」依莉諾心想：「不知道會有多討厭她！」

隔天早上，露西向依莉諾吹噓斐洛夫人有多鍾情於她。

依莉諾還沒來得及回應，愛德華便走進房內，三人都尷尬極了。依莉諾向他打招呼，露西則是在一旁盯著依莉諾，後來依莉諾決定讓他們獨處，自己去找瑪麗安。

p. 86–87 約翰見到妹妹後，想要邀請她們到北國莊園住個幾天。但芬妮斷然拒絕，說：「你有這種的想法，我太訝異了。我才剛邀請史帝爾姊妹來家中作客呢，妳妹她們過幾年以後再說吧。」

約翰同意了，於是芬妮邀請露西和她姊姊前來。露西對於這個接近愛德華的大好機會可是非常開心呢。

幾天後，潔寧絲夫人從女兒帕默夫人家中返歸，帶回最新的八卦。

「愛德華跟露西已經訂婚已經超過一年的消息，竟然讓芬妮生病了！訂婚這事本來只有安妮知道，現在因為她們姊妹住在你們哥哥家中，安妮那笨蛋竟告訴了芬妮！結果芬妮跌落階梯，哭天喊地。史帝爾姊妹還立刻被下了逐客令，因為斐洛家要愛德華娶有錢的摩頓小姐。我倒是不同情他們，受不了勢利眼的人！」

現在話題圍繞在愛德華身上，依莉諾知道妹妹一定會很氣他，便決定先告訴她事情的真相。

p. 88–89 瑪麗安詫異地聽著，不停地流淚，愛德華簡直就是第二個威洛比嘛！

「妳知道多久了？」她問。

「四個月前，露西在巴頓就說了訂婚的事，不過我答應要保守祕密。」

「這段日子妳都為此傷神，卻依然照顧著我，怎麼受得了呢？」瑪麗安驚呼。

「這是我該做的。我不想影響他人。」依莉諾答。

「四個月了耶！妳還愛他嗎？」

「愛啊，可我也愛家人。對愛德華，我毫無怨懟。他們會成婚，到時，愛德華也會忘記他曾看過比她更好的女人。」

「我好像也開始懂妳的想法了，自制力對我而言，不再那麼難以想像了。」

「我知道，妳一直認為我缺乏感情。這件事悶在我的心上好幾個月，卻無法告訴任何人。告訴我這件事的人，也親手摧毀我的幸福。她視我為敵人，想打倒我，不停說著愛德華的事，而我一邊裝做不在意愛德華了，一邊還得忍受愛德華母親的無禮和不友善。現在妳總算知道我多痛苦了吧？」

p. 90–91 「喔……依莉諾，」瑪麗安大聲說：「我之前對妳真是太壞了！」

姊妹倆相擁，痛哭了起來。

翌日，約翰．戴西伍來訪，他說：「我想妳們已經知道，我們驚訝地發現了什麼了吧。」

她們安靜地點點頭。

「妳們大嫂與她母親都氣壞了。我們待史帝爾姊妹她們不薄，換來的卻是欺騙！芬妮真希望當初邀請的是妳們。斐洛夫人叫愛德華去見她。我為我接下來要說的事，先和妳們說聲抱歉。我們勸他取消和露西的約定，只要他娶摩頓小姐，每年就能拿一千英鎊，但他就是不肯。斐洛夫人揚言一毛錢都不給他，還要讓他在社會上無法立足。」

「天啊！」瑪麗安驚呼：「這可真糟！」

「妳們的訝異是正常的，」約翰對妹妹們說：「他的固執真是可怕。」

p. 92-93 「斐洛先生的行為真是正直啊！」在一旁聽的潔寧絲夫人大聲說：「他一定會遵守與露西的婚約。」

「女士，我尊重妳的意見，」約翰答道：「但像斐洛夫人這種有錢的好女人，是無法認同兒子與門戶不登對的女人私訂終身的。斐洛夫人要愛德華永遠滾出家中，不要再見到他，他也真的離開了。到時候遺產應該會由羅伯特繼承吧。弟弟變有錢，他則淪為窮鬼，真慘。」

約翰．戴西伍走了，剩下指責斐洛夫人的三個女人，一致溫暖支持著愛德華。

隔天早上，露西捎來一封信。

戴西伍小姐：

聽聞我與愛德華的苦難後，身為真摯好友的您，知道我們現在過得很好，一定很開心吧！多謝老天讓我們相愛，無畏地經歷許多困難。昨夜與他長談兩小時，我願與他取消婚約，還他自由之身，但他斷然拒絕，表示不在乎母親的怒火，只要我愛他就好。

生活不會很順遂，但也只能往好的地方想。之後他會去教會，希望您能舉薦個可以提供他工作的人。另外麻煩您替我轉告親愛的潔寧絲夫人，盼她也不要忘記我們，還有問候約翰先生、彌德頓夫人、他們的孩子們與我敬愛的瑪麗安小姐。

露西．史帝爾 敬上

p. 94–95 依莉諾知道露西會想讓潔寧絲夫人讀她的信，便立刻拿去給她。老夫人讚賞露西溫暖的心腸說：「她叫我親愛的潔寧絲夫人呢！我真希望能盡力替他找份工作！」

戴西伍兩姊妹待在倫敦已超過兩個月了，瑪麗安準備好要回去，她想家想得兇，依莉諾也是，但她擔心回去的路程太遠。幸虧，帕默一家邀請潔寧絲夫人和戴西伍姊妹，到他們聖摩賽特的家作客，那裡離巴頓只有一天路程。

她們接受了邀請，打算留在帕默家停留一個禮拜。

幾天後，布蘭登上校來找依莉諾，説他替愛德華找了個工作。

「對斐洛先生而言，這至少是個開始，」他繼續説：「那裡的牧師工作輕鬆，還有屋子住，只是房子比較小，而且一年只有兩百英磅的收入。」

依莉諾向上校道謝，承諾會向愛德華報告這好消息。

p. 96–97

一位謙遜的作家

珍．奧斯汀並不追求作家的名氣，實際上，她避之唯恐不及。但原因不是出於害羞或謙虛，而是由於英國十八世紀社會對女人的約束。不論是由工作、政治或藝術而進入公眾領域的女人，都會受大眾負面抨擊，被視為「失去珍貴女性特質」的一群。由於此偏見，在本書初版與再版時，都沒有印出她的姓名。初版僅神祕地指出作者「是位女性」，再版則是直接寫為「《傲慢與偏見》的作者」。

珍．奧斯汀懼怕被知道是位作家會帶來的社會影響，所以每當在家寫作時，她都躲在門後，好在有人接近敲門時，就快速藏起手稿，假裝在做別的事。

儘管這個方法能讓奧斯汀保有私人生活，免於眾人嚴厲、帶有偏見的目光，但一位提出女性議題的作家，卻得默默無名地生活，這看來不免有些諷刺。令人遺憾的是，奧斯汀本可成為其他女性作家的模範，然而她得選擇在她刻劃與批評的社會下，成為服膺社會規定的人。身為女性作家，她證明了自己與當代其他傑出的男作家，同樣的聰敏、見解獨到，具有智慧。

[第五章] 返回巴頓

p. 98–99 離開倫敦前，依莉諾拜訪哥哥約翰與芬妮。約翰對布蘭登上校替愛德華找的工作很有興趣，將她帶到一旁說：「跟妳說件事，斐洛夫人雖然不贊成妳和愛德華的戀情，但她寧願妳當媳婦，也不要露西．史帝爾，可惜現在都太遲了。」

羅伯特．斐洛忽然走進房間。依莉諾之前僅見過他一次，覺得他這個弟弟是個沒腦袋的自大狂，這次碰面，討厭的感覺又加深了。他口沫橫飛説著自己要繼承愛德華財產的事，嘲笑愛德華變成住在小屋裡的窮牧師。

「我對母親説，」他說：「親愛的夫人，如果愛德華娶這年輕女人，我就永遠不見他了！要是早點認識這村姑，我就會叫他甩掉她！」

依莉諾慶幸自己不用留下來，希望永不再見到羅伯特．斐洛。

p. 100–101 他們花了兩天，才到達位於克里夫蘭的聖摩賽特的帕默家。瑪麗安比平常更不安，因為這裡離威洛比鄉下的家只有三十哩呀！她打算獨自走走，沉溺於傷感中。

布蘭登上校也是帕默家的客人，多數時間都與依莉諾討論他要修繕德拉佛的牧師小屋，好讓愛德華入住。他頻繁與她搭話，次數多到她不禁猜想是否約翰說中了，布蘭登上校真對她有意思。然而，她依然感覺，上校和她談話時，心裡想的是瑪麗安。

瑪麗安在濕冷草地上散步兩夜後受寒了，她全身發熱痠疼，但自認只要好好睡一覺就行，堅持不服藥。

然而隔日，她症狀更嚴重了。依莉諾請來醫生，診斷這是感染，幾天就可痊癒。

p. 102–103 數日過去，醫師每日來診，情形依然相同，但依莉諾還是懷抱希望。在給母親的信中，她絕口不提任何瑪麗安病重的消息。

晚間，依莉諾守在妹妹床邊，瑪麗安忽然起身大喊：「媽媽來了嗎？」

「還沒，」依莉諾藏起擔憂回答，扶著她躺下。

「拜託叫她快點來，」她大聲哭喊：「不然就要永別了！」

依莉諾嚇壞了，立即找來醫生。布蘭登上校也連夜駕車，到巴頓接戴西伍夫人。

醫生抵達時，承認用藥無效，感染更嚴重了。依莉諾盼母親能及時到達，見到垂死的女兒最後一面。

但隔天中午，她燒退了，依莉諾開始希望妹妹能熬過去。醫生再來看診時，恭喜瑪麗安在慢慢復元了。當天夜晚，依莉諾因妹妹脫離險境而睡得很香甜。

p. 104–105 早上八點左右，依莉諾聽見前門有馬車聲，急忙下樓要迎接母親，卻看見威洛比在客廳，她擔心地向後退了幾步。

「戴西伍小姐，我想告訴妳一些事。」威洛比請求。

「請說快點，我沒時間！」她不情願地答應了。

「第一，妳妹妹脫離險境了嗎？」

「我想是的。」她冷冷地回答。

「太好了！我聽說她生病了。我是想為自己的行為作解釋，我並不是一直都如此渾蛋的，希望妳妹妹會原諒我。」

「瑪麗安早就諒解了。」

「真的嗎？」他急切地說：「我還是想解釋。第一次相遇，我只想在德文島郡找個玩伴而已。我債務甚多，原打算娶個有錢女人，卻發覺自己愛上了瑪麗安。我想跟她求婚時，親戚史密斯老夫人卻發現我做的壞事，」他慚愧地轉開身說：「可能妳已從布蘭登上校口中得知。」

「我聽說了。」尷尬的依莉諾說。

p. 106–107 威洛比繼續說：「史密斯夫人爆跳如雷，終止對我的資助，拒絕再見我。我痛苦萬分，我知道如果真娶了瑪麗安，我會變很窮，所以只好到巴頓小屋告別。見她又傷心又失落，我真是於心不忍。」

一陣靜默後，依莉諾對他溫和些。

「瑪麗安的信讓我心如刀割，我愛她的程度，遠超過愛我的未婚妻。」

「記住你已是有婦之夫了。」依莉諾說。

威洛比大笑地說：「我結婚了，是啊！葛瑞小姐看見瑪麗安上一封信時，妒火中燒，逼我寫傷人的信給瑪麗安以作懲罰。」

「你已做出選擇，」依莉諾冷冷地說：「尊重你的妻子吧。」

「我夫人不值得妳同情，和她在一起根本不可能快樂，要是我恢復單身⋯⋯。」

依莉諾不悅地皺了眉頭，讓他住嘴。

「我該走了，」他說：「但妳妹妹的婚姻會是我永遠的夢魘。」

「你已失去她了。」依莉諾說。

「可終究會有人得到她的。」威洛比說完便離去。

p. 108–109 半小時後，女孩們的母親驚恐地進門。依莉諾告訴她好消息，戴西伍夫人寬心地哭了，布蘭登上校心中大石放下，默默在旁陪伴。

瑪麗安一天天痊癒，戴西伍夫人總算有機會告訴依莉諾其他消息。在從巴頓來的長途車程中，布蘭登上校忍不住向戴西伍夫人表明對瑪麗安的愛意，盼能向她求婚。戴西伍夫人確信他的好人品，暗自希望瑪麗安到時會應允。

一個禮拜的時間，瑪麗安已然康復，並立即返回巴頓。搭布蘭登上校的馬車回家時，依莉諾欣慰地見到妹妹又回到以往活潑熱情的模樣了。

幾天後，瑪麗安向依莉諾懺悔說：「我行為不檢，與威洛比玩得太瘋，無禮地對待別人。親愛的依莉諾，我對妳也很不好，只在意自己心碎，卻忘了妳也一樣痛苦。」

依莉諾深呼一口氣，將威洛比與她的談話一句不漏告訴她，瑪麗安不發一語，淚水滑落她的臉龐。

p. 110–111 當天夜晚，瑪麗安對母親與姊姊說：「依莉諾所說的事讓我看開了。我看清他的所作所為，我根本不會幸福的。」

「跟那樣的渾蛋在一起會幸福？」母親驚呼：「這不是我的瑪麗安！」

「妳很理性地思考呢！」依莉諾說。

「我怎會這麼蠢！」瑪麗安高聲說。

「都是我的錯，」戴西伍夫人說：「早該嗅出他的不良意圖。」

巴頓的生活恢復了平靜，依莉諾等待愛德華的消息，卻出乎意料地，由母親的男僕湯瑪斯口中得知：「斐洛先生結婚了。」

瑪麗安看見姊姊的蒼白臉龐，不禁哭泣。戴西伍夫人手忙腳亂，不知該安慰哪個女兒。她將瑪麗安帶到隔壁房間，再急忙回來。只見依莉諾詢問湯瑪斯說：「湯瑪斯，誰告訴你的？」

「我親眼見到的，他和之前那位史帝爾小姐在一塊。她從馬車中探頭叫我，詢問瑪麗安身體狀況，之後還說她上次在德文島郡就冠夫姓了。」

「斐洛先生也在馬車上嗎？」

「是啊，就在旁邊，但我沒看見他的臉。」

p. 112–113 「斐洛先生看起來高興嗎？」依莉諾問。

「開心，女士，非常開心呢。」

湯瑪斯退下後，依莉諾和母親不發一語地坐著。戴西伍夫人替女兒感到難過。

過了幾天，一輛馬車停在門口，依莉諾以為是布蘭登上校，結果卻是愛德華。

她對自己說：「保持冷靜。」

愛德華有些蒼白緊張，他進入屋中，戴西伍夫人親切招呼與恭賀他，他則臉紅地喃喃自語。

駭人的寂靜襲捲整個房間，戴西伍夫人只好打破沉默，問候斐洛夫人是否安好。

「斐洛夫人在德拉佛嗎？」依莉諾鼓起勇氣問。

「德拉佛？」他訝異地說：「我母親在倫敦。」

「我指的是你的新婚妻子。」依莉諾說。

遲疑一會兒，愛德華說：「你說的……或許是我弟弟的新婚妻子吧。」

瑪麗安與母親同時訝異地說：「你弟的新婚妻子？」依莉諾說不出話來。

「是的，」愛德華說：「我弟娶了露西・史帝爾小姐。」

p. 114–115 依莉諾奪門而出，喜極而泣，愛德華見她跑開，追了上去。

女士們一陣錯愕驚喜。等她們全坐下喝著茶時，愛德華請求戴西伍夫人同意他和依莉諾的婚事。夫人同意了，而他成了世上最快樂的男人。

「要是母親早讓我選擇自己想從事的職業，那愚昧的婚約就不會發生了。我本以為自己戀愛了，直到遇見妳後，才明白大錯特錯。」

大家開心極了。愛德華解釋，羅伯特本是為了逼露西取消她與愛德華的婚約，才登門拜訪。但露西發現，羅伯特才是繼承財產的人，而非愛德華。兩人臭味相投，互相吸引，便私自閃電結婚。

愛德華的母親嚇壞了，最終卻只能無奈地接受事實。她雖然不認同依莉諾和愛德華的婚姻，依然給了他們一萬英鎊。有這筆錢，他們能盡快成婚，搬到德拉佛的牧師小屋中，成為世上最幸福的一對。

p. 116–117 嫁去德拉佛後，距離並無疏遠依莉諾與妹妹的感情。瑪麗安十九歲時，她心懷溫暖的友情和尊重，答應嫁給從前認為又老又乏味的布蘭登上校。

布蘭登上校也和大家一樣幸福。瑪麗安對他的感情與日俱增，如同對曾經的威洛比那般深愛。

戴西伍夫人仍住在巴頓小屋。瑪格麗長大後，懂得跳舞與宴會，便去拜訪約翰先生和潔寧絲夫人。深厚的家族情誼聯結起巴頓與德拉佛兩地。依莉諾和瑪麗安與丈夫感情和睦，彼此卻還是非常親近，時光流逝，感情不減反增。

Answers

P. 34

B ❶ generations ❷ inheritance ❸ fond
❹ widowed ❺ ambitious

P. 35

C ❶ (c) ❷ (a)

D ❶ F ❷ F ❸ T ❹ T

P. 74

A ❶ company ❷ bachelors ❸ vulgar
❹ calm ❺ intentionally

B ❶ (a) ❷ (b) ❸ (a)

P. 75

C ❶ (c) ❷ (b)

D ❸ → ❶ → ❹ → ❷ → ❺

P. 118

A ❶ T ❷ F ❸ T ❹ T

B ❶ (a) ❷ (b)

P. 119

C ❶ (b) ❷ (a)

D ❷ → ❶ → ❸ → ❺ → ❹